Saved by the Monarch

DANA MARTON

First published in Great Britain 2010
Large Print edition 2010
Harlequin Mills & Boon Limited,
Eton House, 18-24 Paradise Road,
Richmond, Surrey TW9 1SR

© Dana Marton 2009

ISBN: 978 0 263 21585 4

Harlequin Mills & Boon policy is to use papers that
are natural, renewable and recyclable products and
made from wood grown in sustainable forests. The
logging and manufacturing process conform to the legal
environmental regulations of the country of origin.

Printed and bound in Great Britain
by CPI Antony Rowe, Chippenham, Wiltshire

DANA MARTON

is the author of more than a dozen novels and a winner of the Daphne Du Maurier Award of Excellence. She loves writing books of international intrigue, filled with dangerous plots that try her tough-as-nails heroes and the special women they fall in love with.

When not writing or reading she loves to browse antique shops and enjoys working in her sizeable flower garden where she searches for "bad" bugs with the skills of a super spy and vanquishes them with the agility of a commando soldier. To find more information on her books, please visit www.danamarton.com. She would love to hear from readers and can be reached via e-mail at DanaMarton@DanaMarton.com

To Princess Judi.
Long may she reign.
With many thanks to Allison Lyons.

Chapter One

Today he would meet his bride. Prince Miklos hurried along the narrow passageway. If all went well, in three months they'd be married. Given the political climate of the Valtrian kingdom, a traditional engagement in the public eye that lasted a full year wasn't an option. The Royal House of Kerkay desperately needed the positive publicity and all the goodwill a royal wedding would bring. They needed it quickly.

There came that noise again. His attention focused on his surroundings. He wasn't alone in the catacombs, the narrow corridors carved into stone that crisscrossed most of the city and culminated in a jumbled labyrinth under the Valtrian royal palace. Unease prickled his skin, a distinguishable sensation from the goose bumps the cool, damp air gave the prince every time he walked through here. Which wasn't often. But today his schedule was tight and he didn't want to waste time on the reporters who loitered around the palace entrances armed with pointed questions about the unrest in the south.

The lights flickered, but that wasn't unusual. The electric system down here was over fifty years old, currently scheduled for maintenance. He strode forward without hesitation, his military boots making a hard sound on the stone that echoed, mixing with the scrape of other footsteps up ahead.

Some of the catacombs under the city had been turned into a tourist attraction, with guided tours twice a day, but the closed-off section under the palace was guarded twenty-four seven. He expected a palace guard would pop around a corner in seconds.

Except that didn't happen.

Odd. Whoever was down here with him had to have heard him by now. A guard would have come to see who he was, would have properly greeted him. The sound of footsteps grew more faint, definitely not coming closer. Someone in a hurry. To get away from him?

The lights flickered again.

And he considered how he hadn't come across a single guard yet. He picked up speed, but couldn't catch sight of anyone, the footsteps always just around the next corner.

"Halt!" he called out, the intonation that of a military man—he was a Valtrian Army major.

The palace guard would have recognized his voice and obeyed.

Instead, the footsteps quickened.

He took off running toward them, then pulled up short when the lights went out and he was suddenly enveloped in complete darkness.

Ambush, his military-trained mind said. He stole forward slowly, taking care to soften his steps.

His hand moved to his sidearm, although, realistically, he didn't expect much more than an opportunistic tourist who had somehow gotten past a chained gate. Gotten too far while the guards were doing something else somewhere else. The catacomb system was vast.

He stepped to the side and put his back against the wall, ready for anything. But when the lights flickered on for one second, he found the corridor empty in front of him.

And yet his senses told him something was off. He slipped his gun from its leather holster and hadn't taken two steps forward when the lights went out again.

He could be walking into a trap—side tunnels frequently interrupted the corridor he traveled. He moved forward one slow meter at a time, preparing for whatever was to come next, cautioning himself to restraint. A prince beating up a lost tourist would make for terrible publicity, so he bade himself not to jump to conclusions and rash actions when he caught up with whoever was down here. But he kept his gun out, although he didn't take the safety off, not yet.

He followed the sound, turned when he had to, going by feel through twisting corridors in the darkness, enveloped by damp air and musty smells. Then the footsteps suddenly died.

He strained to listen, but couldn't hear anything. He braced his left hand against the wall to orient himself— the stone in the various passages was cut with different techniques, as the catacombs had been added to over the centuries—touched something wet, pulled his hand back.

In some places the walls were moist. There was even a small underground stream, but that was at least a mile from where he was standing.

Could be a water pipe was leaking somewhere beneath the palace. He would have to have that investigated.

He moved ahead, but could no longer pick out any sound beyond the muffled ones he made. The lights flickered back on again. He immediately knew where he was and turned the corner toward the palace entry he'd been headed for. He turned another corner, strode down another long walkway, then another. And spotted a guard, at last, by the steel security door.

"Your Highness." The man snapped his heels together and pulled his spine ramrod straight, staring ahead.

"Has anyone come up this way?" he asked.

"None, Your Highness."

"You're the first guard I've seen since coming in through the stables." He'd entered the catacombs through the secret door at the royal stables at the foot of Palace Hill.

"I'll alert the captain immediately."

"See that you do. Are the lights working properly?"

"Yes, Your Highness."

"They keep going off and on down there."

"It'll be seen to. Is there anything else, Your Highness?" The man's face was set in stone, but his voice betrayed his nerves. His unit had been caught derelict in their duties by none other than a member of the royal family.

And Miklos didn't feel like going easy on him. He was a military man through and through who considered his duty sacred. "Tell the captain I want a full sweep. There might be unauthorized personnel down there."

If the man was surprised, he didn't show it. A complete sweep of the catacombs was rarely conducted. The last time they'd done a full survey was over a decade ago, for architectural reasons. They were testing the rock bed for stability before beginning renovations on the East Wing of the palace. Before his father's death.

He left the guard behind and walked up the stairs, was greeted by another guard as he entered the palace proper. He checked his cell phone when he passed the man. Three unanswered calls from the chief of security. Cell phones didn't work down in the catacombs.

He checked the times for the calls. All in the last ten minutes. Since he was already late for a meeting, he didn't immediately return them. He crossed a receiving area and came out by the library, walked straight through and into the business offices, into the private meeting room where Chancellor Hansen was waiting for him.

"Your Highness."

"Chancellor." He nodded, hating that he was two minutes late. "Go ahead."

"Are you hurt, Your Highness?" The man was staring at his left hand.

And when Miklos brought it up, he realized why. His palm and fingers were stained with blood. He hadn't felt just groundwater seeping through the stone down in the catacombs when he'd leaned against the wall.

The full sweep would tell him what was going on. Miklos would make sure to check in later with the captain. He turned into the small bathroom off the office, left the door open as he pumped soap and thoroughly washed. "I'm fine. I would hear your report."

The chancellor knew better than to push with questions, and gave his usual twenty-minute update instead, leaving ten minutes at the end of their weekly appointment for questions and answers as he always had. But when that was over, uncharacteristically, he didn't immediately take his leave. He was fidgeting, shuffling papers in his appointment book.

He decidedly lingered, although he was the type to plow through his report with the force of a steam engine then be gone, rushing to the next item on his endless to-do list. He had a propensity for believing that he single-handedly kept the kingdom running.

He probably wasn't too far off the mark.

"Is there anything else?" Miklos asked.

The chancellor closed his leather-bound folder softly and looked up with trepidation on his lined face. "The queen is…" He drew a quick breath. "The queen is…" Moisture gathered in his eyes under lids that drooped with age.

"The queen is dying." Miklos said what for most of the country was still unthinkable. He, himself, hadn't said it out loud until now, although he and his brothers had been aware of it for some time, communicating with half sentences and long looks of regret. "My mother is dying," he said it now, again.

The chancellor hung his head.

"Dr. Arynak is requesting audience?"

"Yes, Your Highness."

But the good doctor had asked the chancellor to break the news first. At another time, in a different situation, Miklos would have smiled at that.

Dr. Arynak never delivered bad news to any of the members of the royal family. He had an aversion, more of a phobia, perhaps going back to his predecessors, some of whom had been beheaded for being the harbinger of bad news during the less enlightened centuries.

His evasive techniques, which he took to the extreme at times, could be annoying. He was an excellent physician, however.

"I'm so sorry, Your Highness."

Miklos's heart darkened. The weight that had been straddling his shoulders for the last couple of months now slid to settle firmly in his chest. *How long?* He wanted to ask, but for that he had to wait for the doctor's audience.

"I'll see him as soon as we get back from the airport."

"Yes, Your Highness." But the chancellor didn't look relieved for being done with delivering the doctor's message.

"What else?"

"Have you talked to the chief of security?"

"Not yet." Miklos's voice picked up some impatience, which he regretted. But what could be worse than the queen's impending death? And the country in the worst turmoil already. He was tired of the political fires they were fighting at every level of government.

And still the chancellor wouldn't talk.

"We must leave momentarily," Miklos reminded him.

"There seems to be a plot to assassinate the

crown prince." The words came in a rush, with a pained expression on the old man's face. And anger over the audacity that anyone would want to harm the royal family. And unease because he was treading on the security chief's territory by reporting that information first.

Information that made Miklos's head reel. "Arpad?"

The man in the catacombs… It had been a man; the footsteps gave that much away. Probably young. He'd been fast, and there hadn't been any shuffling. Miklos looked at his left hand. No trace of the blood remained. His body went still for a moment when he thought… Alarm and urgency filled him as he asked, "Where is my brother now?"

"Meeting with a team of security advisors."

He acknowledged the brief moment of

relief and headed for the door. "Where? And why am I not there?"

"We have another appointment."

He stopped in his tracks. How could that slip his mind even for a moment?

He appreciated that the chancellor said "We," even though he spoke of a burden Miklos alone must bear. "I should still go and see my brother." He glanced back.

"But Your Highness…" The Chancellor paled. "You must receive her."

He wasn't in the mood for *musts*. "I must nothing. Am I not still a prince?"

"Which is exactly the reason." The chancellor took a tone he'd employed often during the princes' childhood, using it for the same argument once again—duties of royalty.

Which hadn't chafed in a long time, but they did now, when his mother and brother needed him, and Miklos had to go on a side trip to receive some girl he hadn't met in twenty some years, all because protocol demanded. He almost told the chancellor that protocol be damned. Then reminded himself that a Kerkay never shirked any duty of the crown.

In an hour's time—two at the most—he would be rid of the girl, and he would be back at the palace. He glanced at his watch. "Where is the meeting?"

"The Map Room. Shall I come along, Your Highness?"

"I'll only be a moment." He glanced at his watch again. "You should probably start getting ready."

The Map Room was called as such not only because the floor displayed the map of the world in various colored granite, but because the shelves housed all the royal maps that had survived the tumultuous centuries of Valtria, starting with an outline of the country's hills and rivers, hand-painted on scraped sheepskin in the tenth century.

His five brothers looked up as Miklos entered.

"We weren't expecting you," Arpad, the crown prince, said with obvious pleasure in his voice, although Benedek and Lazlo—the twins—looked rather guilty.

"The chief of security and the rest of the advisors aren't here yet." Janos stated the obvious. He was a prominent economist and involved with politics, as well. His face showed the shadows of sleepless nights.

"And yet you're all here," Miklos remarked, glancing at the old leather-bound book Janos had shoved behind his back as Miklos had entered but now was pulling out again.

Not *the* book?

Miklos put a scowl on his face, regretting that none of his brothers was easily intimidated. "No," he said with emphasis.

"The times are calling for—" Lazlo, a brilliant entrepreneur and born gambler, started to say.

Miklos cut him off. "When were you going to tell me about this?"

"Tonight." Arpad leaned against the fifteenth century massive walnut desk. "We thought you were, er, otherwise engaged?" His right eyebrow slid up, an amused look on his face.

"Leaving momentarily," Miklos said with utmost restraint. "You can put that book away. I'll take care of this with the security chief. You'll be safe, Arpad, I swear to that."

Arpad was a colonel in the air force, but he was the crown prince and could not be part of the kind of foolishness that had been cooked up, no doubt, by the youngest princes. Arpad was to be protected.

Miklos was the only other one with military training among the six brothers. He was the one who was involved with state and palace security anyway. "The Brotherhood of the Crown is a legend," he snapped at them.

"A legend that is about to be resurrected." Lazlo was grinning from ear to ear. That one had way too much taste for adventure.

But all of them, Miklos noticed, looked rather pleased with themselves. They were looking at this as a chance to have some fun, a great change of pace from the sheer dullness of palace protocol and state duties. He hated to be a drill sergeant all the time, but their wild ideas did need someone to corral them.

Not that he didn't feel just a twinge of excitement, looking at the beat-up book.

The story had been his favorite in his boyhood. He and his brothers had spent endless time acting out the glorious deeds of the Brotherhood on the back stairs of the palace, in the secret garden and in the catacombs. But what had been grand entertainment for young boys was surely not a worthwhile discussion for grown princes.

"The queen is not well," he reminded them. And from the way their faces turned somber, he knew that they, too, had heard the latest news about their mother.

"That means the country needs the Brotherhood now more than ever," Janos countered with a dark look.

Miklos drew himself straighter and deepened his frown, then stifled an impatient growl when none of his brothers looked like they took him seriously at all. "We have other duties. Real duties," he pointed out.

"You can trust the military with protecting our family and the country. If you want to escalate things, we can always bring in General Rossi," he offered, aware that his words lost some of their conviction.

His brothers didn't miss a thing. Now they were all grinning. Damn, but they knew they had him. They were circling him already, never mind that there were only six Kerkay brothers, unlike the eight original princes of the Brotherhood of the Crown who had banded together two hundred years ago, a secret society to protect the kingdom during civil unrest and outside manipulation. The story of their wild adventures had been spread far and wide. And was vastly exaggerated, no doubt. But they were the heroes of every Valtrian boy for the past two centuries.

Lazlo formed a fist and extended his hand

into the middle, always first into mischief. Benedek went next—the twins were always on the same page. Then Istvan, a cultural anthropologist who really should have known better, put his fist in. Then Janos. Then Arpad. And Miklos felt himself swept along in the spirit of the moment. In any case, he had to be in. God knew what trouble they would get into without him.

"Duty and honor, our lives for the people and the crown." They swore as one the oath of the Brotherhood, their voices deep and strong, amplified in the cavernous room.

Then Miklos broke up the circle, mindful of the time. The next second, the chief of security was coming through the door.

Janos shoved the book into his waistband at his back and greeted the man with a nonchalant expression. "There you are. Any news?"

Miklos stayed another minute to listen to

the sordid details of the plot against his eldest brother and the kingdom. What had emerged kept him preoccupied all the way to the airport in the royal limousine.

And then, God help him, they were there.

For most of his life, his arranged marriage was a distant thought. So distant, in fact, that sometimes he completely forgot about it until he was reminded by the chancellor's annual report about the girl his parents had hand-picked for him at the moment of her birth.

He was a prince of Valtria, second in line to the throne. He knew all about respon-sibility, had always known this day would come, had always been careful to keep out of deep entanglements. But knowing that he must one day marry for the good of the crown, and stepping out of the royal ceremo-nial limousine at the national airport to receive his future bride, were not the same.

Arpad was the crown prince and the eldest. He'd been supposed to marry first. But that agreement had fallen apart two years ago, and Arpad had been dragging his feet since, putting off selecting a new bride.

"Splendid, Your Highness, splendid." The chancellor beamed now in full ceremonial regalia. He had found a minute to change to give the occasion its due before they left the palace.

That much velvet could not be good for a body.

Being an army major, Miklos was spared the frills and allowed to wear his military dress uniform to the momentous occasion, which he'd donned at his rooms at the military base before coming up to the palace.

"She's an excellent choice, Your Highness," the chancellor said for the hundredth time, probably sensing the prince's hesitancy and working hard to dispel all last-second doubts.

He was downright cheerful, as if their conversation at the palace a short while ago had never happened. His smile fitted the occasion. He always fitted the occasion. Rose to it, by God, come hell or high water, and age hadn't slowed him any. He had served, in one position or another, since the queen had been crowned at the age of twenty-nine, forty years ago, the year Miklos had been born. The chancellor had been a constant part of the six princes' lives as much as their parents, had always been loyal, always on their side against the media, critics, political slandering, whatever.

Which was why his excitement over the arrival of Lady Judit Marezzi felt a lot like betrayal.

"Her background is spotless. A very

sensible woman. As soon as she is tried and tested in situ, and you've had a little time to spend with her, the official announcement can be made. If all goes as expected."

Did that mean it wasn't a done deal? Miklos perked up a little.

"I already have the press releases ready to go."

Resignation defeated hope.

Close to forty, he was used to freedom. And he had more than enough responsibility on his hands; he didn't need the addition of a wife and all the drama that went with it.

His parents, the king and queen of Valtria, had presented a picture-perfect marriage on ceremonial occasions, but life had been far from heavenly at the royal palace. Theirs, too, had been an arranged marriage—for the sake of alliances—that would have been perhaps better off left unarranged. The princes' childhood had plenty of rough spots because of that.

He watched the press, cameras lined up in the distance. The time and place of the arrival had been leaked to a few favored sources in an attempt to control coverage while not appearing as if they were completely shutting the public out. But given the riots in the south, he'd hoped the paparazzi would have better things to do today. The political climate of the country was at the moment somewhat chaotic.

"Odd that she should choose to show up now to claim her due. At the worst possible time," he said, hoping that the chancellor would have some insight about why she'd suddenly decided to come.

The man watched him for a moment. "I suppose there never is a right time to lose one's freedom," he responded simply, warm sympathy in his gaze.

Which was one of the many reasons all the princes loved him. He understood what went on inside a man just as well as he understood what went on inside the palace.

"I expect that things such as this are different for the young ladies," the old man observed gently.

And Miklos felt a sudden shot of guilt for not having considered that she'd probably been planning this day and her wedding for a decade. If not two. Girls were like that.

"Maybe her arrival will save us. If the union goes well, if the people get behind this marriage, it might have the power to stop civil war yet."

Miklos considered the truth in the chancellor's words as he returned his gaze to the Valtrian Airline Boeing Airbus. The stairs were at the door and the red carpet rolled out. The ceremonial army guard stood to line her path to the limousine, keeping the paparazzi back. General Rossi had insisted on the guards to honor the occasion.

Like the chancellor, General Rossi had always been a major source of support for the royal family. He was the reason Miklos had entered the army. Rossi had been his mentor for longer than he could remember.

Miklos scanned the plane. "Tell me again why she refused the royal carrier?"

"She isn't officially a princess and a royal person yet, Your Highness. Maybe she's eager to enjoy the last few weeks of her civilian life. It might be better this way. People might appreciate seeing her for the first time as an average person. She could become the people's princess and all that."

Or not. England had had one of those. Everyone knew how tragically that had worked out.

"This better not be an indication that she's going to buck protocol every chance she gets," he said tight-lipped, so that the cameras recording him from afar wouldn't catch his words. "God knows what sort of liberal upbringing she received in America."

She was twenty-nine, an age that suddenly seemed too young for him to comprehend. What could she possibly know about life? At least she would know all about Valtria and its royal customs and heritage. Her people would have seen to that. She would know what was expected of her. But would she do it?

Why wouldn't she? He pressed down on an unexpected wave of unease. If she weren't prepared to do her duty, she wouldn't have come here.

Some movement showed at last at the plane's door. The military band struck up Valtria's national anthem. Two little girls dressed in white formal dresses appeared out of nowhere with a spectacular bouquet of Valtria's signature purple roses, their national flower. Judging by the chancellor's pleased expression, he had arranged that.

Miklos stood ramrod straight, not a twitch betraying his impatience. He wanted to be done with his official duties of meet and greet and get back to investigating just who'd been down in the tunnels with him earlier. He didn't have to worry about Lady Judit feeling neglected. Her weeks were booked touring the palace and country with a receiving committee, meeting everyone who counted, interspersed with only brief visits from him. They would have enough time to get to know each other once they were married.

The airplane's door opened, a flight attendant appearing first as she pushed the door to the side with a nervous smile on her face.

Followed by Lady Judit Marezzi—his future princess.

The first thing he noticed was that she was not, in fact, a girl. She was a stunning woman, a thousand times more beautiful than the snapshots in the chancellor's reports. Waves of auburn hair reached to the middle of her back, glinting bronze in the sun. She was lithe, her movements graceful, her simple ivory dress accentuating her feminine figure.

His suppressed reluctance eased a notch.

Then he noticed the shock, surprise and confusion on her face as she looked at the receiving line. There was no greeting smile, no little wave, no pose at the top of the stairs for the cameras as was customary on state arrivals. In fact, she clutched her oversize handbag as if she were ready to bolt. Almost as if…

As if she hadn't expected him to be there at all. Almost as if all this was a surprise to her.

WHEN IN ROME, DO AS the Romans do. Judi looked down the stairs, took a deep breath and moved forward, aware that a planeful of weary travelers waited to deboard behind her. Maybe Valtria always went all out for arriving tourists. She only wished, as she walked the red carpet, that when she'd been bumped up to first class she hadn't received the first seat in the first row. She wouldn't have minded if another passenger was first off the plane, somebody who'd been here before and knew what to do.

Then she reached the ground and two adorable little girls came to curtsy before her and hand her an enormous bouquet of the most gorgeous pale purple roses she'd ever seen. Cameras flashed, reporters shouting in various languages. She recoiled from them as she caught a few questions in English, "Why now?" and "What are your plans?"

Which pretty much told her that there was a misunderstanding of giant proportions going on here. Either that or she was on some hidden-camera show, but for the life of her she couldn't think who would set her up like that.

She was a little cog working at a large company that made video games. In other words, a complete nobody.

A portly, official-looking man stood at the end of the red carpet in front of a black stretch limousine. He was smiling from ear to ear, looking at her, his outfit straight out of some Renaissance painting, wearing enough velvet to do Elvis proud. But it was the military official next to him who drew Judi's attention. He looked vaguely familiar.

His dark eyes watched her with disquieting intensity. He was a head taller than the man in the funky robes and filled out his uniform in a way that could make a girl sigh. The way he carried himself meant he was the man in charge. He had a charismatic smile that made looking away from him nearly impossible. If all Valtrian men looked like him, she might have a pretty interesting holiday yet.

More men in uniform lined her path. If it weren't for the red carpet, she would have thought this was all some sort of security measure and the handsome stranger the security chief. As it was, she figured there had to be someone important on the plane, a celebrity even, and tried to think back to her fellow passengers in first class. Then glanced back. The two guards who'd been standing just outside the airplane's door when she'd stepped out were still there, holding everyone else back.

Her steps faltered right in front of Liberace

and the army guy. Their smiles widened as they looked at her expectantly.

She was pink-eared embarrassed. "I'm sorry. I don't think I'm who you think I am," she whispered to them and looked for a way to gracefully disappear. Sadly, a trapdoor on the tarmac did not conveniently present itself.

Liberace looked confused. Army guy looked as if he might have expected her to say something like that.

But before he had a chance to respond, Liberace inclined his head and said, "Your Highness, may I present the Lady Judit Marezzi."

The air stuck in her lungs. And stayed there permanently when his Highness—his Highness?—took her hand and brushed a warm kiss over her knuckles. Oh my God, he was! She recognized him from media photos now, although the Valtrian royal family was never as big news in U.S. tabloids as the British. But because of her Valtrian roots, the few times they had been mentioned, she'd paid attention.

His lips were utterly masculine and bone-meltingly sexy, and might have twitched, whether with annoyance or amusement she couldn't tell.

"Welcome back to Valtria. I hope your flight was pleasant." His voice was low and rich timbered, a voice made for seduction that reso-nated in her chest and seemed to nestle there.

She didn't breathe again until he let her hand go.

Liberace looked up to the airplane. "And your social secretary and entourage?"

Entou—what? Her head was beginning to spin.

"I'm sorry, there must be a mistake." She offered a painful smile, hating to make a fool of herself in front of the handsome prince. Oh man, the stories she was going to tell the girls at the office when she got back.

His Highness caught on first. He nodded to one of the guards next to him, who opened the limo's door. She was ushered in efficiently, away from the flashing cameras and the most awkward public moment of her life. It bordered on ridiculous how grateful she felt for the reprieve.

The two men got in after her and, for a moment, tense silence ruled.

Then Liberace said, "I've sent a detailed outline of the reception, protocol and hour-by-hour plans of your entire stay to Lady Viola, your social secretary." He seemed bewildered and scandalized by her behavior.

His Highness simply observed her. And managed to unnerve her completely just by doing that.

Her brain slowed to a crawl. "Aunt Viola?" She stared at the older man. Her aunt had just had emergency gallbladder surgery. Judi would have canceled the whole trip if her aunt hadn't forbidden her to do it. The only time the short, timid, fairy godmother-type of a woman had ever put her foot down as long as Judi could remember.

"Who do you think I am?" she asked tentatively.

"Lady Judit Marezzi, daughter of Lord Conrad Marezzi and Lady Lillian."

Okay, the names matched. Except for the lord and lady part, although she did remember her father mentioning to her they were from an old, important family. She didn't remember her mother, who had died when Judi was three. She did remember her father, however. He'd gotten remarried, to an American, before dying just days after

Judi's fifth birthday. Her American step-mother wasn't the type to dwell on the past. Neither was Aunt Viola, who'd moved to the States after her father's death.

The limousine began to move. And for a long while, as Liberace went on about impossible and incomprehensible acts, she was frozen in place, unsure what on earth was going on and how to act. Then the car left the airport and entered a busy highway, and she was aware all of a sudden that she was being carted off to an unknown location by two strange men.

"Stop." She raised her hand, palm out. "I need you to let me go right now." Where was her luggage, anyway? Never mind. She would take that up with the airline later. Right now she needed to return to reality posthaste. "I want you to let me out right here."

His Highness flashed her a somber,

I-don't-think-so glance. She appreciated the manly, sexy and formidable look on a guy as much as the next girl, but not when said guy was standing in the way of her freedom.

"Now listen—" She might have wagged her index finger for a second there before she caught herself and found her very last smidgen of ladylike restraint.

Liberace gasped. "Please consider… The press… This is… We are miles from the city proper."

"And who are you?" She was running out of patience.

He looked puppy-eyed hurt. "I'm Chancellor Hansen. You might recall that we *have* corresponded."

Uh-huh. And she kept in regular touch with Mick Jagger and the Dalai Lama, as well. She was beginning to feel on the edge of desperate.

"I need you to take me to my hotel. I'm staying at the Ramada at center city." She dug into her purse to get the paper with the exact address.

DID SHE THINK SHE WAS in a taxicab?

"You'll be staying at the royal palace," Miklos said. Security would be impossible at a hotel. If that was what she wanted, she should have notified the chancellor months ago so they could have properly set it up.

"I don't think so." She gave him a look full of attitude. Her lavender eyes shone like jewels.

The chancellor sucked in a sharp breath.

Miklos cocked his head as he took in the woman. He wasn't used to his word being questioned. Definitely not in the military, where a superior officer's word was the law, and not in civilian life, either.

She was pretty but it would only get her so far with him. He happened to have too much on his plate today to deal with her drama and theatrics.

The four younger princes—Janos, Istvan, Lazlo and Benedek—were better at diplomacy than the two eldest. Arpad, the crown prince, and Miklos were more of cut-to-the-chase type of men. "If you have no interest in honoring our parents' agreement, then why are you here?"

"As a birthday present to myself." She sounded and looked thoroughly exasperated. "I thought it was time I discovered my roots a little," she went on, then paused and looked at him with full-on suspicion on her beautiful face. "What agreement?"

He cast a sidelong glance at the chancellor, who was now looking positively ashen.

"Our *engagement.*" He said the last word

with emphasis so there would be no way she could misunderstand him.

Her nearly translucent skin lost all color. "A what?" she asked.

Chapter Two

He didn't have time for this.

"Aunt Viola?" Miklos drew up one eyebrow as he glanced toward the chancellor. The future princess's companion and social secretary seemed to have been amiss in her duties. To say the least.

"Lady Viola Arynak. A distant relation to Lady Marezzi," the chancellor supplied, looking thoroughly off balance.

"Arynak?" Foreboding filled the prince.

"Dr. Arynak's cousin."

Which might have explained a lot. Was she also averse to delivering bad news? Had she left the princess's engagement out of her education altogether? Although he couldn't comprehend why anyone would think of the prospect of being married to him as bad news.

"Engagement?" she asked again, color returning to her face. She had the fine features of Valtrian aristocracy and lively eyes that made it near impossible to look away from her.

"An agreement was reached between our parents at the time of your birth, then reinforced at the time of your leaving Valtria." When her father was appointed Valtrian ambassador to the United States.

She really had an attractive mouth. Even when it was hanging open.

"I was two when my family moved to America. You—you pedophile!" Outrage shook her voice.

"I was not quite thirteen at the time and

wasn't given much say in the matter," he said mildly. "You came up to my knee and hugged it. The families took it as an agreement." She'd been a charming toddler, large blue eyes that had turned lavender over the past decades and curly red hair that had grown into auburn waves.

She flashed him a look of contempt.

Far from the look of adoration she'd regarded him with back then. He hadn't known what to do with her, felt lucky that protocol required nothing but a short introduction. He'd been relieved that she was so young, that the alliance he was expected to make with her wouldn't have to happen for endless years yet. Two decades had seemed an eternity to his thirteen-year-old self.

But that particular eternity had just come to an end. And his fond fantasies of an obedient wife who toed the line and understood the responsibilities of the monarchy were rapidly coming to an end with it.

The fire in her eyes was something to behold. "This is the twenty-first century. You can't be serious," she admonished him.

He didn't even answer that. Duty was everything to him. That she would question hers the moment she was required the first small thing annoyed him to no end and didn't fill him with optimism regarding his future wife's character.

He would marry her anyway. He was prepared to make that sacrifice. She could be key to uniting the country again. Her father had been an extremely popular lord and political figure, a son of the Italian minority living in Valtria. Her mother had been a descendant of the Austrian-related branch of Valtrian nobility. Her marriage to him would be far more than just a happy occasion for all the people to come together at last and celebrate. Their joining would be symbolic, could even start the country on the path of healing ethnic wounds if it were played in exactly the right way.

"I'm an American citizen. I got that when my stepmother adopted me. You can't make me do anything I don't want to do." She threw him a so-there look that was haughty enough for a princess while also incredibly hot.

"Valtrian-American," he corrected and wondered if that, too, might not have some use yet. She'd spent most of her life outside the country. She had no alliances yet, no preferences, no past here to dredge up. She could be seen as a fresh breath of air to the royal family, impartial, sympathetic to all the people of the kingdom. Something to discuss with the chancellor when they had a sane minute.

His cell phone rang. Under normal circumstances, he wouldn't have picked it up in the lady's presence, reserving his full attention for her. But at the moment, he was glad for any diversion from the disaster their meeting was turning into. Seeing the chief of security's number on the display made his decision for him.

"What happened?"

"Two bodies were found in the catacombs. Palace guards." The man's voice was grave and apologetic at the same time.

"Procedure followed?"

"Yes, Your Highness. Emergency procedures for the possible infiltration of the palace are being put in place. The royal family will leave for a weekend hunting holiday to Maltmore within the hour."

He loved Maltmore, a fine hunting castle, had fond childhood memories of the place and

Monsieur Maneaux, the Frenchman who had taught the young princes sword fighting there. Under the current situation, to remove the royal family to the castle from the royal palace for a few days was the best course of action.

Which was going to be questioned by the media, since it had been unscheduled, but the chancellor would come up with some innocent reason. Maybe even involving the arrival of Lady Judit.

"Very well." His ancestors had built Maltmore in the foothills of the Alps, a location as majestic as it was well defensible.

But also a hundred miles from the capital. Which meant he would have a hard time investigating the goings-on at the royal palace from there. "I shall be staying in residence." The rest of the "Brotherhood" could just investigate from the safety of the castle walls. Actually, that suited him pretty well.

"Your Highness, I must advise—"

"I shall be staying in residence with the Lady Judit." The perfect excuse for him to lag behind his family.

The prince and the future princess are getting to know each other. Courting.

The press would turn it into something mushily romantic, and nobody would guess the dire situation at the palace, news of which could not come out under any circumstances. With all the upheaval in the country, the supposed Freedom Council that worked to bring down the monarchy would capitalize on information like that, use it as proof that the people were fed up with the royals. The council would gain more power, and their power was even now almost too much to handle.

His mother was ill—she had to leave. His brothers, if they stayed, wouldn't be able to help themselves, but would try to investigate and look for any excuse to perform some heroic deed. He could never hope to keep an eye on all of them. They were better off at Maltmore. But he should be able to keep a close eye on Judit. How hard could it be to keep track of one young woman? And the monarchy's enemies didn't know her yet anyway. She wasn't a target.

"We'll talk when I get there." He hung up the phone, then addressed Lady Judit. "I'm sorry, but your official schedule will have to be changed."

Under the circumstances, maybe it was best if she weren't out there, prancing around the countryside. He'd see to it that she would be kept busy at the royal palace, while guarded heavily. They might even spend more time together than originally planned. He found that he didn't altogether mind that prospect.

"I don't have an official schedule." She glared at him.

The chancellor drew up his shoulders and shook his head, nonplussed. He seemed completely out of sorts and taking this mix-up badly. He probably felt responsible.

"If we were engaged all this time like you say, how come you never contacted me? If I hadn't decided to come here, would you have just forgotten about it and let it all go?" Judit asked.

"I've been busy. I've been patient, trying to give you the time you needed." And relieved that she'd stayed away, to be truthful. He had a full life, a career in the army, a pretty busy schedule. It'd always seemed that they would have plenty of time yet. Which led the chancellor to his ultimatum. Might as well tell her some of that.

"If I hadn't made arrangements before my

fortieth birthday—" he felt a moment of embarrassment "—you would have received an official contact from the royal family that requested your presence here. Chancellor Hansen would have organized the confirmation of our engagement."

"When is your fortieth birthday?" she inquired.

"At the end of summer."

"Procrastinate much?" She actually looked amused for a second.

His turn to glare at her.

"I think you want this as little as I do," she observed.

"I want to do my duty." That was all he ever wanted. Whatever it took to help the country and the monarchy. When one was a prince, personal feelings did not figure into the equation.

"I don't want anyone to marry me out of

duty," she snapped, as if offended. But then she added on a softer voice, that suited her much better, "Can you understand that?"

"Lady Arynak mentioned none of this to you?" Miklos asked.

NOT REALLY. JUDI SAT ramrod straight on the leather seat, not allowing her shoulders to slump. *Don't let them see you scared.*

The limousine felt smaller than a Mini Cooper. The prince had what could be called an imposing presence, his intense energy filling the space and then some. Grainy pictures in tabloids were one thing. Sitting face-to-face with all that charisma was vastly different, heaven help her.

She wondered for a second if anyone had ever naysayed him. That probably didn't happen too often. A man like him wouldn't be used to resistance from women.

"My aunt is a sweet old lady." She sounded defensive even to her own ears, but couldn't help it. She loved Aunt Viola. Who *was* sweet. Too sweet, even. She had a tendency to say whatever anyone wanted to hear. But, hello, that was exactly why she was so very likable and had a gazillion friends.

"She did bring up from time to time that I should visit Valtria." But Judi had always put it off, focusing on her studies at first, then on her career. And her aunt *had* mentioned marriage, urged her more and more often lately to consider that it might be time to start thinking along those lines, but Judi had been reluctant.

Not that she was commitment-phobic, although she'd been accused of just that by more than one ex-boyfriend. But it did seem that everyone she'd ever truly loved always ended up dying. Her mother when Judi had been three, her father when she'd been five, her stepmother when she'd been ten.

Maybe she *was* scared to fully fall in love and commit to a man. And her aunt hadn't pushed or played matchmakers like older family members or some of her friends. She just wasn't the pushy kind, which Judi very much appreciated. Having someone like Aunt Viola by her side was wonderful when life was filled with one harsh reality after another.

Like the fact that her parents had sold her out to some prince when she'd been a toddler!

He seemed annoyed but held it in check and remained studiously polite, a man who fully knew the meaning of aristocratic restraint. Which she appreciated. He was overwhelming enough as it was.

"Look, we're both adults. We should be able to figure something out." There had to be something she could say to make him see how absolutely crazy this all was.

He watched her as if trying to see inside her. "The country needs our alliance," he stated simply.

His very presence demanded that she curtsy and say *Yes, Your Highness*. But in addition to her Valtrian heritage, she also had her indomitable American stepmother's spirit in her. She called on that.

"That's not up for negotiation." She did her best to remain calm and match his cool demeanor.

Her father had been a high-profile political figure, then her stepmother after him. They'd both been dragged through the mud. If there was one thing she'd known for sure at an early age, it was that she would never become a public figure when she grew up.

"If I can make the sacrifice, why is it that

you cannot?" His masculine, sensuous lips flattened. "A true daughter of Lord Marezzi would never refuse her duty."

I would and I will—just watch me, Buster, she wanted to say but had a feeling that she would get better results by remaining civil and rational. She needed time. *Delay.* "I believe we really need to talk about this. I'm going to need time here. And a lot of questions need to be answered."

He watched her darkly for a long moment. "Agreed."

So he was willing to negotiate. It saved her from having to jump from a moving car and run for the hills. She felt a small sense of relief, the first since she'd gotten off the plane.

"You will consider the situation?" His face remained impassive, but his eyes betrayed that he wasn't too happy with her.

Not that she was all that thrilled with him, either. "Yes." The situation she would consider. Marriage to him, she would not.

Even if he wasn't that bad to look at: raven-wing black hair and dark slate eyes, a straight, aristocratic nose and a powerfully built soldier's body. Which, really, she should have been too angry to notice. It annoyed her to no end that she had. So he was handsome. So who cared?

He was archaic.

An arranged marriage. In this day and age? Who was he kidding?

Maybe he was crazy. Not a raving lunatic, but slightly off. Madness ran in the royal bloodlines of several European countries; she remembered that from history class. Just her luck. A whole, perfectly fine country, and the first person she ran into was their off-his-rocker prince.

They slowed for a sharp turn. She opened her mouth to talk some reason into the two men, but what happened next froze her. She watched the scene unfold, her body immobile from the terror she felt.

Two cars plowed through traffic and pulled to a screeching halt next to their motorcade. Two men got out. One pointed a grenade launcher at the limo behind them that was supposed to carry her entourage but was empty instead, save for the driver. The guy blew it to pieces.

Just blew it up without warning.

Fire shot to the sky.

Car parts rained to the pavement.

She might have screamed. She couldn't hear her own voice, deafened by the explosion.

The guy pointed the grenade launcher at their car next.

If she'd had command of her limbs, she

would have been hiding under the seats by now.

The prince opened the door and got out with murder on his face to confront the armed men. He stood tall and straight, focused on the attackers. "This is not necessary. I will come of my own will and listen to your demands." His voice was clipped, betraying the restraint it took for him to just stand there.

He let himself be disarmed, but with enough tension radiating from him that she thought his control might break at any second and he would attack. She felt disconnected from the whole scene as if she were watching it on a movie screen. Her mind was numb with shock.

"No further violence is necessary." His voice was tempered steel.

And for a moment, she wasn't sure

whether he was trying to convince the attackers or himself.

"I'll go with you. We leave them here," he stated.

"Everyone's coming." One guy kept his gun trained on the prince while another reached in and yanked Judi from the safety of the limo.

Faced with a grenade launcher, she didn't have it in her to resist. She went like a rag doll.

The chancellor scampered to the far end of the expansive seat and wedged himself in. They would have needed a crane to move the man. The attacker pointed the grenade launcher at him.

She caught the prince shift on his feet and get ready to make his move, so she prepared to duck, knowing all hell would break loose in a second. But then, unexpectedly, the ceremonial army guard opened fire. Bullets pinged off the pavement and the cars.

The kidnappers gave up on the chancellor, and Judi was unceremoniously shoved into the back of a van, along with His Highness. Then the van took off, the attackers returning fire, swerving all over the road so badly that she banged against the van's side.

She grabbed on to the one thing available for leverage—the prince. She could feel the flexing of an impressive amount of muscle under his military jacket, but there was no time to appreciate that now. The van swerved as bullets exploded all around it.

"Oh God, oh God, oh God."

She'd been wrong, she thought. The prince wasn't the only nut in the place. The whole country was insane.

She so should not have come here. She yelped as the gunfire intensified. She could see little in the dim van, the prince's wide chest pretty much filling her field of vision. She prayed that the bullets wouldn't break through the back door and hit them. She hung on even tighter as he put an arm around her and braced them with his feet to stop from bouncing. He held them both safe by sheer strength and will.

She was not impressed. All she could think of was that she should have gone with her first idea and celebrated her twenty-ninth birthday in Puerto Vallarta instead.

HIS HANDS WERE TIED behind his back and he was blindfolded, but his feet were free, so Miklos walked his prison to get a sense of it. When he bumped into something, he turned around to feel it. A chair. Which he catalogued as a possible makeshift weapon before he moved on.

"Where are we? It's freezing," Lady Judit asked from somewhere nearby.

"Up in the mountains." He had no idea beyond that. The van had had no windows, and the men had blindfolded them before taking them out of the vehicle and into a building. He figured about two or three hours had passed since their kidnapping.

"The country's security forces are out in full force looking for us. And probably most of the army. General Rossi would see to that," he said to reassure her. "Lady Judit—"

"For heaven's sake, can you at least call me Judi?" she snapped.

She really did have a difficult nature. "Judi. Please do not fear. I'm going to protect you." A prince remained valiant under all circumstances. A lesson drummed into the six Kerkay brothers from early childhood by the chancellor.

She snorted.

Which drew him up short. He didn't think a true princess would snort. Yet he couldn't deny that he kind of liked her irreverent, spirited nature. *Heaven help him.* He *would* have been able to appreciate—he corrected himself—an irreverent and spirited nature in about any other woman, but not his bride, who would be a princess of the kingdom.

He moved forward and bumped into a table, thought about Chancellor Hansen. Worry filled him for the old man. There'd been a gunfight after he and Judi had been thrust into the van. He wondered how the chancellor had fared.

"Why did they bring us here?" she was asking.

He wasn't sure he should tell her. But the fact was, she was here now, her life in jeopardy because of him. She deserved to know. He finally reached a wall and moved alongside it, turned his back to feel for a window with his tied hands.

"I was informed this morning that there's an assassination plot against my brother, the crown prince." As if Arpad hadn't had a rough-enough month already. His chopper had nearly gone down two weeks before, due to malfunction. He'd been on his way to a ceremonial troop inspection. He was lucky he was still alive.

In hindsight, fresh suspicion arose that the accident could have been planned. But no, a special investigative team had gone over every last screw of the chopper after the incident. Miklos had read their report. Thoroughly.

"I'm in the army. Of the six princes, I'm the most involved with security. Could be whoever is behind the plot wants me out of the way so it'd be easier for him to get to Arpad."

A long silence followed his response. Then, "Why am I here?"

"You were in the wrong place at the wrong time," he said with regret.

"Funny, but I've had that feeling ever since the plane landed," she said in a droll tone.

The corner of his mouth twitched up. Her sense of humor was refreshing. And she stayed relatively composed under duress. She hadn't become hysterical at any point during the kidnapping—another trait that might come in handy for a future princess. Which she refused to consider, and for a split second he wondered if he could afford to let that whole issue drop. He hadn't really wanted a bride. He wanted a reluctant bride even less.

And she was nothing like the duty-bound daughters of the Valtrian aristocracy. Whoever he married wouldn't simply be his wife—she would be a princess of the country. She would have endless duties and responsibilities. And she would be expected to fulfill every last one of them. She would be expected to make sacrifices for the people.

If he were the only other person involved, he would have been willing to respect her explicitly worded wishes in the matter. But their union went beyond him; it involved the whole country. And despite some misgivings on his part, he couldn't give up his hopes for their grand peacemaking alliance. The country needed that.

"I'm truly sorry that your introduction to Valtria is like this. It's a wonderful country. I wish your arrival could have been different."

"You and me both," she groused, then asked, "Why do the people want the crown prince dead?"

"Not the people. Some people. Three businessmen in particular." The three men who led the so-called Freedom Council. "We have three major ethnic groups in the country: Italian, Hungarian and Austrian. There are some businessmen who would like to destroy the monarchy, divide the country along those ethnic lines and make their own republics." How little she knew about the country was truly disappointing.

"Which would be led by these powerful men?"

At least she was catching on quickly. "Right. Each would have a small republic. They could then rewrite the laws to suit their best interests, anything."

"Why?"

"More power. More money. When Arpad takes over, he's changing the country to a constitutional monarchy. Already, preparations are being made. The next step after that is joining the European Union. That will change everything. Not all EU regulations will be favorable for all current Valtrian business practices.

"The bottom line is, for the Freedom Council the time is now or never. It's easier to take out the royal family now and gain control of the country than try to take out a whole parliament once constitutional monarchy gets here."

"Don't the people understand that they're being manipulated?"

"There's a lot of propaganda out there right now to create tension along ethnic lines. That's all people see." He felt such regret over that, and wondered if, not having grown up in Valtria, Judi could understand.

"For as long as I can remember, we were

simply Valtrian," he explained. "Now everyone is seeing themselves as Italian or Hungarian or Austrian, and century-old grievances are being dredged up."

"The whole divide-and-conquer thing. And political instability brings economic instability, of course," she added.

So she did get it. He went on, encouraged. "The economy is suffering already. And the Freedom Council is doing its best to convince the people that it's because the upkeep of monarchy is too expensive."

"You've said Freedom Council more than once. What is it?"

"That's what the rebel leaders are calling themselves. Pretty ironic, actually. Under their mercenary government, the people would be anything but free."

She remained silent for minutes. "I wish I knew more about Valtria."

"How much were you told of our history?"

"My father used to talk to me about it. But he died and—I was too young to remember."

"And your aunt Viola?"

"For the most part, she just tried to convince me to move back here. Gently," she added. "She doesn't like to say things she knows I don't want to hear."

He rolled his eyes beneath the blindfold.

Then he turned his head toward the door when he heard it open.

Something clanged to the floor.

The door closed again.

"What do you think that was?" she asked.

"Food." He hoped.

And got a sudden idea just as she asked, "What are we going to do?"

"Escape," he answered. "But we'll have to get the blindfolds off first." He moved toward her. "Keep talking so I can figure out where exactly you are. Just say something. Anything."

"For my thirtieth birthday I decided to visit the country of my ancestors and discover my heritage. At the airport I was kidnapped by a deranged prince—"

"Greeted by an eager groom," he corrected as his head bumped into hers.

"Then I was kidnapped by other deranged men," she finished.

"What, that wasn't in the brochure?" He made an attempt to lighten the mood between them. "People pay extra for extreme vacations like that."

Then his lips were on her cheeks, her skin silky soft. And they both fell silent.

He ignored the heat that flashed through him and zipped straight to his groin. He moved his mouth up to the blindfold, grabbed the material with his teeth, breathing in her exotic flower scent. She held herself ramrod straight.

"Relax. I'm not trying to seduce you." And just for the hell of it, he added, "Yet."

But he could envision it in crystal-clear detail all of a sudden. Her tangled up in his sheets. Naked. Under him.

"I don't want you to confuse me with those women who throw themselves at the feet of handsome princes."

Disappointingly, her voice held no trace of passion. Instead, he got the distinct impression that she was mocking him.

"You're in no danger of that." He pulled the blindfold off all the way at last. "Your turn," he said, waiting impatiently to see again.

A moment passed before he could feel her velvety lips on his left cheek, an inch or two above his mouth, next to the blindfold. Her firm breasts pressed against his shoulder as she leaned into him. She moved her mouth. The blindfold moved next, a scant centimeter only before it slipped from her teeth. She had to fit her lips to his skin again.

He didn't mind the delay.

Then the blindfold was off at last, around his neck. She looked up, and they were nose to nose, her lavender eyes staring into his, her soft breath fanning his face.

"At least you think me handsome. That's a start, I suppose." Utterly ridiculous how pleased those words she'd let slip made him feel. A foothold, that was what they were. Something he could stand on while he fought to gain more ground. Courting a woman couldn't have been that much different from conducting a military campaign.

She blushed a brilliant red, right to the tip of her ears. The response was so charming, he couldn't help but smile at her. Maybe he was gaining ground already.

But she was gathering herself fast, her eyes narrowing, her mouth opening, no doubt with a snappy comeback. He couldn't let her spoil the moment. He couldn't give up the ground he'd gained; he wouldn't give up an inch. That was not the path to victory.

So he leaned forward and kissed her.

Her lips were even softer than her cheeks, although she immediately pressed them together and pulled back. He followed and dragged his mouth across hers.

Her instant rejection of him on her arrival had injured his masculine pride, whether or not he was ready to admit that, and some part of him pushed to prove something to her, although he couldn't have exactly said what that was.

All he knew was that he wanted her to look

at him with something other than the ever-present disdain in those mesmerizing lavender eyes. Their arranged union was important. It had a purpose. They had roles to fulfill. He wanted her to consider that.

He was still intent on conquering when his eyes closed on their own. And in the next instant he was seduced by her softness and her scent. She was unlike any proper noblewoman he'd ever known. He had no idea what to do with her.

But a very clear and detailed image of what he *wanted* to do with her readily flashed into his mind. It would not have been the smartest thing at the given moment, nor in compliance with protocol.

All of a sudden, he felt as if he'd been starved for the taste of her for years, had been waiting for her. The meeting of their lips, the physical connection between them, was startling. He had expected to enjoy kissing her, but the sensations taking over his body went way beyond that.

Instant heat.

Instant need.

There was absolutely no way she could deny it, although he knew she would try. He didn't even mind. He was looking forward to going a couple of rounds with her before she gave in.

He had no doubt in his mind that she would see reason eventually. The draw was too strong between them. He was prepared to pursue her until she accepted him.

Too soon, she twisted away. Her face was flushed, her eyes deep lavender pools.

He eased out of his focused need, into a teasing smile. "Would being married to me be that terrible?" He was surprised to find that her response would matter quite a bit to him.

She dragged in air, her nostrils flaring. She

didn't much look like the demure young ladies at court as she said in her toughest, meanest voice yet, "Don't you ever do that again."

He drew a slow breath, held it, then let it out as he considered.

"All right," he said brusquely, even as his body demanded more of her. "I won't kiss you again. You do, however," he added, and let the challenge stand between them, "have my permission to kiss me any time you wish."

Chapter Three

Kiss him?

He probably thought he was irresistible just because he was a handsome prince. *Insufferable* was a much better qualifier for him.

"Right after they make a ski resort in hell," Judi snapped, pulling her bottom and feet through the loop of her arms so her hands would be in front. The man was driving her crazy. What had she done to deserve this?

He had the gall to grin at her, a slow and sexy grin that she supposed was meant to show her who was in control.

"Well, then," he said. "Get your camera ready, princess, because the devil will be snowboarding before this is all over."

Then he stood with insufferable arrogance on his face and turned his back, his tied hands at eye-level to her.

"And don't call me princess." God, was that the best she could do? She sounded pitiful even to her own ears.

He was wiggling his long fingers in front of her face. He had strong, masculine hands, she noticed, rough palms that probably came from riding.

"What do you want?"

"I cordially request your assistance in the freeing of my hands."

He was mocking her. She wanted to tell him off, but she did want to get out of here, and she was smart enough to know that he was her best chance. She put her fingers and teeth to work on his ropes, ignoring the warmth of the inside of his wrist every time her lips touched against the beating pulse there.

Not to be aware of him as a man would have been impossible. She had to work hard, every second, to pretend that she wasn't affected by him.

The ropes didn't budge an inch.

"I don't think this is going to work," she said just as the door opened again.

A young woman came in, her shoulders tight-set, her head downcast. Her movements were jerky, as if she were scared. She put a bottle of water on the floor just inside the door without looking up. Then she stepped back out and locked the door behind her.

Judi watched as the prince sat and tried to pull his hands to the front, but he was tied tighter than she was.

She couldn't help him, so she scanned the room again. In the video games she designed, she always hid a secret door or a secret key that the right player could use to escape any dungeon. No such conveniences here.

Miklos abandoned his attempts at getting his hands to the front and walked over to try the door—no luck—then picked up the water with an awkward squat and a blind sweep of his fingers, brought it back and handed it to her sideways.

She screwed off the top with some finagling and lifted the bottle to her mouth.

But he said, "No. Me first."

"Of course, Your Highness." She rolled her eyes, but held the bottle to his lips.

He took a taste, swooshed it around in his mouth, swallowed it, waited a couple of seconds. "Please call me Miklos." Then nodded that she could drink.

And she felt pretty stupid when she realized that he'd been checking the water for drugs or poison. She was distracted enough to put the bottle to her lips without wiping the opening. Which, when she became aware of it, felt oddly intimate all of a sudden.

He caught the look on her face and seemed to be amused. "We have kissed."

"I guess. Sort of." She tried to act like it was no big deal.

A dark eyebrow rode up his forehead. "I don't remember any sort of about it."

He was having fun at her expense.

"Well, it's not going to happen again," she snapped.

He didn't look like he believed her.

But after a moment, he did remove his lethal gaze from her and moved to examine the windowless room while she drank some more. "Next time they open that door, we'll be prepared."

She swallowed and held the bottle out to him so he could actually drink for real, not just a taste. "For what?"

"To break out."

So they took up positions behind the door. Meaning they stood behind the door. He called it "positions." At this stage, she was willing to do whatever he said. Within limits.

"So you're a soldier or something?" She took in his uniform that she hated to admit looked pretty good on him.

"Army major."

"Is that a ceremonial title? They can't make a prince do push-ups, can they?"

"You should have seen me in basic training." He shook his head. "I thought I was a hotshot footballer when I joined the army, daily training, laps around the field, whatever. The first six weeks of training nearly did me in. I think only my pride kept me from running back to the palace."

She was surprised he would confess that. She didn't think he was always this open, not when his every move and every word could be reported in the media. But he'd been acting as if they'd known each other for some time. He let his guard down around her.

She didn't know whether to like that or wish for some stiff royal distance between them.

But she did have a lot of questions about him. So if he were willing to answer, she was definitely ready to ask.

"Why did you join in the first place? As a prince, you probably had your pick of careers."

"Tradition, partly. And because I thought it was the right thing to do. Valtrian young men and women serve our country, ready to sacrifice their lives for it if needed. How could a prince do any differently? At coronations, the people take an oath to serve the monarchy. And the monarch takes an oath to protect his or her people."

"I always thought that sort of thing was only for show. A formality."

His face seemed to tighten. "I assure you that a Kerkay always takes his oath and duty seriously."

Great. Back to the duty thing. He would start badgering her about the marriage next. She should have quit while she was ahead.

But he didn't bring up the engagement, and she was smart enough not to return to the subject of duty again, so for the next few hours, they stood in silent readiness.

Nobody came, although, from time to time, they could hear people passing in the hallway. One complained that there wasn't enough water.

"We've two days' worth. That's all we need," another one responded, then said something about Maltmore castle, and the two of them laughed.

They spoke Italian. Like Switzerland, Valtria had several official languages to reflect its ethnic groups: German, Italian and Hungarian. Plus English was used in the business and entertainment world, as well as being the language of the fledgling tourist industry in the country.

Reminding her of her heritage, Aunt Viola had bribed her into taking lessons in all of Valtria's languages through her school years, but only the Italian had stuck enough so Judi had at least some rudimentary understanding.

She looked at the prince. The two-day thing didn't sound good. What would happen to them then? His face was shadowed, his eyes glinting hard. He looked like he, too, was considering some worst-case scenarios. She didn't dare ask.

Eventually, when no one came, they sat down. Then they ate the food that had been brought in earlier—crusty rolls and cheese—and drank the rest of the water. After a while, the tension in the air eased.

And his attention returned to her. "So you didn't come to Valtria to marry me?"

"Do I really have to say this for the hundredth time?"

"Birthday trip."

"That and a little research."

That seemed to get his attention. "On what?"

"Castles and royalty. I'm working on a new video-game series for kids about a little princess and her dragon. It's going to have a lot of castles with moats."

"Any princes?"

"Not so much. Just the dragon. The games will be fun but educational. Each will tackle a different message appropriate for elementary school children. Friendship, diversity, courage, resilience, that kind of thing."

"Impressive," he said and, for a change, didn't look like he was mocking her.

She hated that she felt ridiculously pleased at his compliment.

A crooked smile split his face. "When I was younger, I used to think that dragons were real. I thought they lived in the passageways under the palace. And since I was a prince, I knew I would be expected to slay them at some point. As a five-year-old, it was pretty disconcerting."

She'd never seen him more approachable or more attractive than at that moment, with his guard completely down, reminiscing. "What happened?"

"My brother Arpad eventually had a talk with me about some facts of life. Dragons, Santa and the Easter Bunny." He grinned.

"Oh." She didn't know whether that was bad or good. When she'd been young, she had loved the whole Santa thing.

"Big relief," he said. "Arpad was a great older brother. He taught me all about the facts of life."

Now things were starting to get interesting. "Girls, too?" She could picture the two teenage princes out on the prowl for a date. God help the kingdom.

"Especially girls." His grin turned wicked.

She felt a flash of heat, but all too soon she was shivering again in her spring dress. She'd been dressed for sunny weather. A thousand feet up, winter still reigned.

"If you can get my jacket off, you're welcome to it," he said.

She took in the military uniform with some longing. Looked warm. Of course, there was no way to pull it off with his hands tied like that.

"I can get your pants off," she said just to keep herself from falling into a self-pity fest and to let him know that she wasn't the least bit intimidated by him.

But instead of laughing her off, he held her gaze. "Go ahead."

And damn if the temperature in the room didn't kick up a notch.

"No, thanks. I wouldn't want you to freeze off your royal behind." If he thought she was going to treat him with deference—which he was no doubt used to—he had another think coming.

In fact, treating him like the guy next door might just be the key to stop being so aggravatingly aware of him. At least some of his magic and power had to have come from the whole prince thing.

He drew up a dark, aristocratic eyebrow.

"I don't want to see your royal behind," she clarified.

"You feel threatened by my behind?" he bantered right back, not looking the least offended by her disrespectful comments.

"Oh, please."

"You don't think you could resist it," he said.

She would not dignify that with an answer.

Which didn't deter him. "You brought it up, so you must have been thinking about it."

Great. Now she was wishing they did have some protocol that mandated proper distance between them. "I don't think dirty innuendoes are appropriate for a prince."

"You'd be surprised at all the inappropriate things princes do when nobody's looking," he said. Very suggestively.

She threw him what she hoped was a baleful look, sucking in her cheeks at the same time to hold back a grin. She really couldn't stand it that she was starting to like him.

Of course, she had bigger problems than that. Like having to use the bathroom. She held it for another half hour before she could overcome her embarrassment enough and mention it to him.

"I'll bang on the door and ask them to let me out. They'll have to." Didn't they? God, she really hoped they would.

"Don't." He got up to pull a plastic snow bucket from under the table that she'd only marginally registered before. He set it in front of her and took off the lid. "I'll turn my back."

She looked at the scratched-up red bucket. "I don't think that's going to happen. I'll ask them really nicely."

"I don't want them to take you out of this room."

"It's just a potty break. What do you think they'll do to me?"

He turned. Held her gaze. His face was the most serious that she'd seen it yet. "Anything they want."

And she had to think about that for a moment and reevaluate whether or not she really wanted to spend some one-on-one time with a kidnapper. "Fine. Turn around."

He walked to the far wall, stopped with his back to her.

"I can't do this if you can hear me," she said after a minute. "Could you…"

He waited her out.

"Maybe plug your ears," she suggested.

"Not with my hands tied behind my back."

"Sing?"

He didn't even shake his head, just broke into some Valtrian song about rain. He had a pleasant, rich baritone for singing. Except when he went all goofy and added an "ooh, baby" off key.

He was certifiably insane, she thought, and now that he couldn't see her, allowed herself an ear-to-ear grin.

With any other man, she would have been tempted to give in to the attraction. She was single; he drew her as no man ever had before. What would have been the harm in a fun vacation fling? If—and that was a big if—they ever got out of here.

But a smart woman did not have a fling with a prince, not without sacrificing privacy and being dragged through the mud by the media. And a smart woman most definitely did not have a fling with a prince she was supposedly "engaged" to. He was arrogant enough to take the slightest softening on her part as agreement.

She sealed and put away the bucket. "Thanks."

He shrugged off her gratitude as he came back to sit on the floor next to her.

"So what sort of adventures does this princess in your games have?" he asked her with a look that made her wary that he was going to read way too much into whatever answers she gave.

"Her castle is kind of like a labyrinth. Sometimes she searches for treasure, some-times she fights monsters."

He drew up a skeptical eyebrow. "Teaching kids about materialism and violence?"

The urge to hit him over the head was pretty strong. "The treasures are something like a song that will play if the child gets the answers to a series of math questions right, or a story she will hear as a treat. The monsters are not vanquished with weapons.

Their names are written on their chest with some letters missing. The kids will guess the missing letters. When they call the monster by its true name, it will disappear. That game teaches spelling."

"Not bad." A speculative look came into his eyes along with some merriment.

And she was sure that he was silently laughing at something at her expense. "What?"

"According to the chancellor, the perfect occupation for a young lady who's to become princess is something that has to do with children. He was very pleased when you started to design children's games."

Right. Aunt Viola apparently corresponded with him and kept him up to date. An exaggerated groan was all the response she would give Miklos.

"So this princess of yours strolls around

in her little labyrinth." He seemed unwilling to let the subject drop. "Is that what you do? Move forward until you see something you're scared of, then you move back?"

"She can move up and down, too." So there. "And some roads are not worth going down. Roads that are obviously dead ends." She gave a pointed glare.

"You think marrying me would be a dead end?" His gaze grew intense, with a dangerous glint in it. "Boring maybe, no more excitement, ever?"

Knowing what she knew of him now, she was betting life with him would be the exact opposite. God help her, she wished she were the princess in her game. She could go up to her highest tower and lock herself away from the temptations of the handsome prince.

She wondered whether he would disappear if she called him by his true name.

She should be so lucky.

THEIR CHANCE TO ESCAPE didn't come until morning. They spent the night—talking and sleeping alternately—sitting back to back, the only way Judi would allow him to give some warmth to her chilled body. If Miklos hadn't been tied, he would have hauled her onto his lap and fully against him anyway. As it was, he was forced to obey her wishes.

Frustration ate at him for more reasons than that. He hated to be stuck here when he should have been out there investigating, protecting his family.

They stood ready when the door opened this time, having heard footsteps approaching.

He leaped and had the man knocked to the ground the next second. Judi was there then, kneeling on the guy's head, mashing his face into the floor before he could raise a shout.

"Check his pockets." Miklos pushed the door closed with his shoulder. "We need his knife if he has one."

Her hands were in front; she had more mobility. The man grunted as she shifted her weight and went for the pockets.

"Nothing." She sounded as frustrated as he felt.

He kicked the man's gun toward her then turned enough to take off the guy's belt. By the time he looked up, she was stuffing an old-fashioned European dinner roll into the guy's mouth. An effective gag, although they could have probably used the food. Judging from the temperature and the length of time it had taken them to get here, they had to be fairly high up on the mountain.

He got the belt free at last. She helped him tie the guy's hands. When they were done, they got up, leaving him grunting and squirming on the floor.

She held the gun in her hands. Gingerly.

He could tell that she was about scared out of her skin, completely out of her element, but she held up well. She knew what needed to be done, and looked determined to do it. He swore silently at their situation, at the rope that bound his hands. He wanted to be able to protect her, and it galled him more than he cared to admit that he could not promise her that he would take care of her.

That he might have to ask her to help him.

"Can you shoot?"

"No." She flashed a small, apologetic smile before nerves pulled her soft mouth back into a tight line again.

"Above your thumb. That's the safety. Push it forward. After that, you just aim and pull the trigger."

She nodded.

He moved to the door first, opened it a fraction, looked out. Nobody in the short hallway. He could see two other plank doors to his left, then a larger door with a small window through which he spied snow outside. A half dozen snowsuits hung on pegs in the hallway, all of them red, striped with black. Not the best for hiding in a snowy landscape. Apparently, the kidnappers didn't anticipate being found and having to run.

"If anyone catches us, you get behind me," he whispered.

Not that he would be any good except as a shield from any bullets fired, but he was willing to do that to save her. She shouldn't have gotten involved in this. Shouldn't have been brought here. Her life was in danger because she'd been in his company. He couldn't forget that.

Wind howled in the mountains loud enough to cover whatever noise they made, but he proceeded with extreme care anyway. He pulled Judi behind him and waited until she closed the door. Then they stole to the window with her covering his back.

Nothing but snow and more snow outside. He opened the door an inch and stuck his head out, looked to either side. A couple of sets of skis leaned against the side of the building, the old-fashioned kind that snapped on any decent boot at hand.

He stepped back with a scowl.

"What's out there?" she asked, breathless.

He reached awkwardly for the largest ski suit and boots, the rope around his hands slowing him down. When he had everything, with some help from her, he hurried outside. "Nothing."

"That's good, right?" She got what she needed for herself without having to be told, and followed him, closing the door behind them.

"I was hoping for a truck with chains on the tires." He waited for her to dress him, which galled the hell out of him. Skiing was going to be interesting. He wondered how long it would take before he fell flat on his face. "Hurry up." He glanced back toward the cabin, but everything there seemed quiet. He tugged on his ropes again.

They had to come across a sharp rock sooner or later, something he could use to fray their ropes. Everything would have been so much easier if they had a car. He could have shifted; she could have driven.

A vehicle would have provided a lot more

protection against the weather and against their enemies as well. As it was, they would stand out against the snow in the colorful suits, easy pickings for a good rifle even from a distance.

The clouds looked black, laden with snow. The wind hurled frozen flakes in the air from what had already fallen in the last couple of days. The temperature was well below zero, the terrain treacherous. They'd had a lot of late spring snow in the mountains in recent days, putting the steep slopes at high risk for avalanches.

He examined the peaks and oriented himself as to where they were. He'd been on enough military exercises up here to know every peak and valley.

"Please tell me there's a ski resort just around the corner somewhere," she said as she dressed.

"The nearest village is about twenty miles from here." As the birds flew—which they couldn't. They would have to go around boulders, go out of their way to avoid gorges, adding extra miles over and over again. "But it'll be the first place they'll look for us. They can easily catch up with us on the path. Or call in reinforcements who could be waiting for us in the village to grab us as soon as we reach it."

He looked at Judi, who was done with her suit—as much as was possible, anyway— and was pulling boots on, ready to do whatever was required, without fussing or whining. Determination put extra sparkle in her lavender eyes.

For a moment, he wished he hadn't made that stupid promise about not kissing her.

"The royal family is at Maltmore Castle,

that way." He gestured eastward with his head. "It's the safest place we can go."

"How far?"

"Thirty miles."

She knew he needed her help without him having to ask, and he appreciated that. Appreciated it even more that she didn't make any smart remark about it, which he'd half expected. She dragged the suit up his legs. His muscles tightened as the back of her hand dragged along his inner thigh. Under different circumstances, this could have been…interesting.

She yanked the suit up his torso, had to stop with it at chest level since he couldn't get his arms in with his hands tied. She zipped it for him as far as she could, same as hers was. The arms of the suit dangled under their armpits.

She was scowling at the sight they presented. "Looks pretty ridiculous."

He merely shrugged in response. "It's about survival, not looking pretty. We need the suits." He shoved his feet into the boots, and she fastened the clasps for him.

He was the type who could take care of himself and was damn proud of that, so needing her didn't sit all that well with him. He should be helping her. He was feeling less and less the valiant prince by the minute.

"I'll find something to cut the ropes once we get out of sight of the cabin. We'll have plenty of daytime hours," he said brusquely.

"Let's get going then." She shot him a look of full-on optimism. "We can do thirty miles in a day. Easily."

On a regular hike maybe, down in the foothills. Not up here above the snow line without a tent or any means to make a fire.

"Sure," he said anyway, because he didn't have the heart to tell her that it would take a miracle for them to make it off the mountain.

Chapter Four

They weren't free an hour before the snow-storm hit. The good news was that he'd been able to get them out of their ropes by then with the help of a sharp rock. He also knew the mountains and had found a small cave. The bad news was that the temperature had to be ten below. And even less with the wind-chill factored in.

So they sat as far from the cave's entrance as possible, out of the way of the wind that had been howling for several hours now. They were both chilled to the bone, the small space not allowing for much movement.

Miklos wrapped his arms tighter around her. For once, she didn't protest.

"Wish we had something to burn," she said, her breath a puff of white mist in the air.

He'd been thinking the same thing, but they had nothing save the clothes on their backs. Another time, another place, he would have been happy to get rid of all their clothes and burn them, he mused for a second, then got his mind out of the gutter.

"So you never received any missives from the chancellor?" he asked to distract her from the cold and himself from his baser instincts that seemed to come alive in her company. She was too beautiful by far, even half frozen. His active imagination readily supplied a dozen ways they could keep each other warm.

"Never," she said with emphasis.

He blinked hard before he realized that was an answer to his question about the chancellor and not to his thoughts.

"Your social secretary must have received and answered them. I got whole folders on you. Once a year." They had not done justice to the woman, though. Nothing in the papers had mentioned that she was feisty and vibrant and that her lavender eyes would be alive with passion—and fury—when he pressed his lips to hers.

Her head snapped up. "Folders of what?"

"Whatever you were doing. I got school report cards. Snapshots."

"You know my grades?"

He grinned. "I know all your secrets."

A storm gathered in her eyes.

"Fine. All I know is that you were better in English than I was. And in math. And that you tried a lot of different hairdos over the years."

"I can't believe Aunt Viola would do this to me. She has a lot to answer for once I get near a phone." A violent shiver ran through her.

If and when they got near a phone, the first call would be to General Rossi, asking for help. "Your father never said anything?"

"Maybe he did and I don't remember, or maybe he was waiting for me to get older." She was looking at her feet, her arms wrapped around her knees, her voice softening. "He was diagnosed with leukemia when I was five, and responded badly to the chemo. Died shortly after his first treatment. I don't think anybody expected that."

She was silent for a long moment, then added, "He did use to call me princess. I thought all daddies called their daughters princesses."

He tried to picture her as a little girl with her father. But the old images of her in his head had been firmly overwritten by the beauty of the woman in his arms.

Five years old.

He'd been nearly thirty when his father had died. And still it'd shaken him, shaken the whole country. His father had been king by marriage, the queen being the true monarch, the one with royal blood. And now the queen was desperately ill. He dared not think what stress would do to her if she ever found out about the plot against her eldest son. He and his brothers had tried to shelter her as much as possible over the past months. They'd been adults for a long time now, well aware of the realities of life, but still every one of them hoped for a miracle.

Judi had been just a small child when she had lost both of her parents.

"That had to be hard, to be orphaned at such a young age." He remembered the sympathy he'd felt for her back when he'd first heard, remembered that there'd been a motion to bring her back to the country, but as her stepmother had adopted her upon marriage to her father, she had full custody of the child. So a companion had been sent who would later become her social secretary and prepare her for her duties when she returned to Valtria to take her place in the royal family. Or so they'd thought.

Apparently the Lady Viola was not the best choice they could have made. She hadn't prepared Judi for her role in Valtria at all. Leaving a future princess unaware all these years about what would be expected of her was nothing short of criminal negligence.

She'd been chosen because she was a distant relative to the Marezzis, not quite the aunt Judi's affections promoted her to, but a third or fourth cousin. In hindsight, a stranger with a better grasp of what was expected of her might have served Judi better.

No wonder she had responded to the news with resistance. Still, he couldn't help hoping that, given some time, he might succeed at convincing her to honor their parents' agreement.

"Would you not consider the engagement for the good of the country?" he said with his arms securely around her, knowing this was neither the time nor the place but unable to stop from pushing her for an answer.

And he already knew she didn't like to be pushed.

"Would you stop badgering me with it? You don't even know me." She was shivering again.

"That could be easily changed." He was

willing to spend time with her. As much as necessary.

"The answer is no. What are you going to do about it? Threaten me with beheading?" She glared.

So cold weather made her grumpy. Something to remember. "Good to see that you still have your sense of humor. This isn't the Middle Ages."

"You can't want this." Her gaze grew serious, her voice earnest. "You can't want me. You don't know me. You're just worried that…" She paused to consider him. "Will there be a huge media scandal about you when I go back home?" Her face was unnaturally white from the cold.

He fought the urge to warm her skin with his lips. He was beginning to seriously worry about her, enough to let the not-wanting-her comment slide.

"Semi-huge. We've had what's called in royal circles a secret engagement, although the chancellor leaked some details to the media the morning of your arrival. There's a balance we must maintain as far as privacy goes—our public wants to feel involved with our family," he explained. "If you leave abruptly, people will just assume that the news was only an unfounded rumor. There'll be some Prince Jilted at First Sight headlines, too, of course," he said just to cheer her up.

And, predictably, she did offer a shaky smile. "That'll be the end of your reputation with the ladies."

"I'll die a shriveled-up old bachelor, likely."

She laughed for the first time since they had met, a clear, bubbling sound that warmed his insides. He hoped it warmed hers as well.

The storm raged outside, an errant gust

swirling snow inside the cave now and then. He wished he could be somewhere like this with her, together, out of the cold, out of danger, just talking, the two of them. He wished he hadn't procrastinated meeting her until the last second. Maybe years ago when they'd been younger and more flexible, the battle lines wouldn't have been drawn so quickly between them.

"As sorry as I am about the damage to your reputation that my leaving might cause, I still would like to go back home when we get off this mountain," she said after a few moments. "Given the circumstances, I'm sure you understand."

He didn't understand at all. Except the part that he was being rejected, his country—which he loved enough to die for at a moment's notice—was being rejected. And that stung.

She couldn't leave immediately. She had to give him time to change her mind, although he could see how the events of the last twenty-four hours might have soured her on Valtria, and he regretted that very much. She'd seen nothing but the dark side, a handful of rebels intent on destruction.

He hoped they would live long enough for him to show her the rest.

He found that he liked her company. She was independent and irreverent, and tough. And beautiful. Her lips were a temptation he was ill-equipped to resist. Especially when they were as close to his as they were at this moment.

She didn't want to marry him. And she was not what one would call perfect princess material. She was too headstrong for that by far. But that didn't stop him from wanting her. He was big on facing any and all problems head-on, and didn't see a point in denying this one, not to himself in any case.

"Can I ask you something?" she asked, then went on without waiting for his answer. "You would have just done it? Gone ahead and married a stranger because that's what people expect you to do?"

"When we next run into the chancellor, ask him about the duties of a prince," he said ruefully.

"How about love?" She was looking directly into his eyes.

He loved that look, the challenge in it, her strength to face down any issue and speak her mind. She employed none of the coy glances and feminine manipulations of the young ladies at court. He appreciated that even when she was asking questions he felt ill-equipped to answer. How about love?

How about it? he wanted to toss back. Or ask if they could discuss lust instead, a topic more within the area of his expertise. But she deserved more than a glib answer.

He could have fallen in love a time or two if he had allowed himself. But he was a man of discipline. "What people want most from the royal family is stability and re- spectability. The commoners have given their blood and sweat for this country over the centuries. The least we can contribute is doing our duty."

"It can't be your duty to marry a woman you don't love." She sounded exasperated and bewildered, scandalized by what she believed was an archaic way of life.

"My duty is to marry a daughter of nobility and have children with her to provide suc- cessors for the throne, should anything happen to my older brother."

A moment passed before she responded. "So you're what, the backup prince?"

He winced. The tabloids had called him that in the past.

"But that's so unfair," she said, her face pale with cold.

"Everyone has their role in life."

She seemed to think on that. "But most people get to pick their role. What they want to do for a living, where they live, who they marry."

He simply nodded. "Well, there's that."

She stared at him as if expecting something more. Blinked. "Don't you ever rebel?" she asked after a minute.

He had, when he'd been a teenager. But his mother and father had always been shining examples of monarchs who loved their people and did their duty and whatever else they could to better the common man's life.

And at one point, he'd come to understand the challenge and beauty of that.

"Lazlo is the rebel prince," he said. "You'd like him."

"And what are you?" she snapped. "Mother Theresa, dedicating your life to the masses?"

If she knew the thoughts he'd had while holding her in his arms, she wouldn't have confused him with a saint. He let his gaze rake over her. Heat gathered between them slowly, tension that had nothing to do with their disagreement on the duties of a prince.

The banked fire inside him burned despite the freezing cold around them. It would have taken little to burst into an open flame. Disconcerting to say the least. A prince was, at all times, in full command of his basic needs and emotions. When it came to ladies, a prince courted, he did not ravish. A prince was not overtaken by out-of-control desires.

So he cooled the heat that had gathered inside him and loosened his arms around her. "Lazlo is the rebel of the family." He tried to pick up their conversation but didn't know what to say beyond this. He had to look away from her, so he looked toward the opening of the cave.

Seconds passed, endless, one after the other.

"Will I meet him?"

He knew what she was asking. Will we survive? He had no business making impossible promises, but he did anyway. "You will."

His thoughts darkened as he wondered how his family fared. Maltmore Castle was somewhere below them.

"But why do your enemies want to harm Arpad? If anything happens to him, you would just take his place, right? Technically, there are five back-up princes. Hurting

Prince Arpad wouldn't end the monarchy." She frowned as she tried to make sense of it.

"The Queen is very ill." From the way her eyes widened, he knew that she understood what he meant. "Arpad could be taking the crown soon. His death would cause a disruption. Chaos, even if it's temporary, would play into the hands of our enemies. All they need is a crack in the wall of tradition, to make people wonder if the monarchy really is necessary. Arpad is the charismatic one. People have been preparing for him to be king for a long time now."

"They might not swear allegiance to you as readily?" She rubbed her hands together. Their gloves were wet, so they had both taken them off.

"No. If civil war broke out...they might not accept me as their new king."

And, God help him, he did not want to be

king. He was happy as a soldier, happy to be protecting his country and his family without having to be involved in politics. But if the unthinkable happened, he would do what was expected of him.

"I haven't spent nearly as much time in the public eye. I spend most of my time on the base. I'm a through-and-through military man." Since it looked like she could barely bend her fingers, he took her hands between his own to warm them.

She didn't protest. Which meant she had to be about freezing to death. Her comments in their conversation were coming increasingly slowly. He knew what that meant, along with her eyelids that were beginning to droop. Hypothermia wasn't that far off. He held her close and prayed for the end of the storm so he could get her off the mountain.

She leaned forward, presumably to rest her

head on her drawn-up knees, but it didn't prove comfortable, he supposed, because she ended up leaning against his chest. Her hair slid aside and revealed the graceful arch of her neck.

He could feel a shiver go through her, and couldn't help thinking that she wouldn't be here if not for him. She would be at the Ramada, sipping cocktails at the bar with handsome men hitting on her by now. He erased that last part from his mind when he found that it prickled. Then he dipped his head and let his lips touch her neck.

"Hey, you said no more kissing." She turned slowly with an accusing glare that was a faint shadow of her regular fiery self.

"Just checking your temperature."

Her eyes narrowed, but she didn't look like she had the energy to argue with him. "I'm freezing."

He held her tighter. "Try to think about

something else. Like the dragon video game that you're making. I didn't know girls were into video games."

"I'm not a girl. I'm a grown woman." She shot him some weak indignation.

"Certainly so. Would never make that mistake. Heard you roar and all that."

A moment of silence passed. She had to be in worse shape than he'd thought. She wasn't even rising to the bait.

"You could put a prince in. You could pattern him after me. Handsome and valorous."

She gave a muffled groan and, after a moment, said, "She has a dragon."

"A pet dragon?" He considered the possibilities.

"A dragon friend."

"She could do things with a prince that she can't do with the dragon."

She shot him a dark look, but the corner of

her mouth twitched up. "It's not an X-rated game. It's for elementary school kids."

"A shame," he said, and was aware that they had moved even closer to each other for heat.

Her lips were inches from his.

The air thickened around them. Her gaze flew to his, filled with alarm and something else. It was the something else he wanted to investigate.

But a deep rumble sounded above them before he had a chance to do anything.

Her look changed to one of panic, and she burrowed her face into his neck as the cave shook around them. "What is that?"

The rumbling got louder. Right on top of them.

"Avalanche," he said, powerless to do anything but watch as snow slid over the opening of the cave from above and buried them, sealing them inside.

HER BODY SHOOK ALONG with the side of the mountain as Judi clung to the relative safety of Miklos's arms. He sat motionless, holding on to her. She could no longer see him, all their light was cut off. But she could feel snow pushing against her, snow that the force of the avalanche had shoved inside their small cave.

"Grab your gloves," he said, letting her go.

She immediately missed his heat, the sense of safety and comfort he had provided. She searched the snow around them, found one glove, but not the other, panicked a little. "I lost one."

"Here." He touched her.

She took the glove by feel and put it on. The rumble quieted as quickly as it started. She could hear snow squishing and Miklos grunting.

"Dig," he said. "On top. As high as you can."

Words could not describe the sense of terror she felt. Her muscles clenched with it. But she made herself move and set to the task gingerly, not wanting to disturb some balance and send more snow tumbling into the cave, which happened anyway.

Her fingers, which had warmed in his hands, felt frozen again once back in the wet gloves. Her fingertips were aching with cold within minutes.

Dig.

Breathe.

Blood pounded in her ears from the effort. Darkness and fear seemed to swallow her up.

"Faster," he said after a while.

She was pretty sure she was going to lose fingers over this. Or more. She was well aware that the odds of them getting out were not good. Maybe if she had a moment to catch her breath, she would regain back some strength. "Can't we rest?"

His voice was tight when he responded. "We're not going to have enough air."

She hadn't thought of that. The fresh panic gave her a shot of newfound energy.

Dig.

Scratch.

Push.

Move. Move. Move.

Her lungs constricted. She gasped for air. Oh, God. She wasn't ready to die.

"Relax." His voice, soothing, wrapped around her in the darkness.

"I think." She gasped in a lungful of air. "We." She gasped again. "Running out of oxygen."

She was beginning to feel dizzy. She could not see the cave walls in the dark, but felt certain that they were closing in. Her movements grew frenzied.

"You're panicking." He sounded calm and sure.

She prickled at that.

"Breathe in slowly. Count to four. Breathe out."

What good did counting do when they had no air? She wanted to shout at him, but when she did slow her breathing, she found that he'd been right. She was breathing easier.

If she weren't frozen senseless, it probably would have irritated her that she was proving herself to be a total wimp by freaking out. Especially since she was going for the whole independent, capable woman sort of image. For the prince's benefit. So he would finally get the picture that she wasn't the type who could be coerced into an arranged marriage.

She cleared her throat and controlled her

digging, changed her efforts from frantic to effective. "How much snow do you think is above us?" She held herself together as much as she possibly could.

"Dig up and out. Right next to my tunnel. We need room to push the snow back." He reached back and adjusted her hands. "Could be one foot, could be a hundred."

She so did not need to hear that. But she was glad he was leveling with her. He obviously thought that she was capable of handling the situation. She prayed that he was right about her. In any case, his trust in her made her want to try harder.

She threw herself into the work, but her fingers were numb, her body stiff from cold. She was losing focus fast, she realized when she found herself spacing out just a minute or two later. Most of her thoughts were now circling around how she could get warm again, instinct pushing her to stop all movement that ate up her remaining energy. All she wanted was to curl up in a ball.

She'd been half-frozen sitting in the cave. Being surrounded by snow on all sides now was bringing her body temperature down rapidly.

She forced herself to keep working alongside him. "Has this ever happened to you?"

She badly needed to hear that an avalanche was survivable. She lived in D.C. What did she know about avalanches? An image of a big, hairy dog with a small barrel of brandy tied around his neck, sniffing snow, came to mind from some old TV show. She didn't think any of those would be coming around. Nobody knew that they were up here.

"Can't say that it has," he said.

She felt like crying—it wasn't as if he

would have seen her in the dark—but she didn't want any tears to freeze to her cheeks. She kept on digging.

The kidnapping had been a shock to her system and utterly surreal, but a quick bullet seemed preferable now to the slow suffocation that she faced here. She could hear Miklos breathing heavily next to her. He was clearing enormous amounts of snow. She knew this because she could feel more and more room ahead that she could keep moving into. Her efforts seemed pitiful compared to his.

They were out of the cave now, in a snow tunnel, going up. He moved in front of her, pushed snow back, and she did her best to shove it down next to her toward the cave, kick it along with her feet. But after a while, the snow behind her piled up, closing them in from that end.

Leaving them with even less breathing space.

Don't stop moving.

Breathe slow and even. She'd read someplace that breathing rapidly used up more oxygen.

She suspected that if it weren't for the air trapped in the snow around them, they would have already suffocated. Air that wasn't going to last long anyway.

They weren't going to make it. The avalanche was too deep. The realization was becoming harder and harder to ignore, her dark premonitions impossible to shake. This was it.

"How are you holding up?" he asked without stopping when she went still from fear and exhaustion for a second.

"Starting to feel claustrophobic." She set to work again, as much as she could. Too slow.

Her fingers no longer moved, so she just pushed her hands around from the wrist like small shovels.

Snow surrounded them.

For a moment she couldn't tell which way was up. She felt a flash of panic again. Then drew a deep breath and calmed herself, listened to the sound of the prince's digging.

Miklos. Right. He was supposed to be above her.

As her mind clicked back on, she realized that she was entering hypothermia. First the brain slows, then the body, then comes death.

"I think we're nearing the surface," he said after another minute.

Her ears were buzzing. "How do you know?" Pushing the words out was an effort.

She could no longer do anything with the snow that he pushed back, just roll against it awkwardly and compact it to the sides of their tunnel, which made the space even tighter. She felt like she was trapped in a coffin made of ice. She spaced out for a moment.

"The snow doesn't feel as packed here." His voice brought her back.

Too late, she thought as a wave of dizziness washed over her a hundred times stronger than before. She was going to pass out. She didn't have the strength to tell him. She didn't think she'd be telling anyone anything ever again. In hindsight, she should have let him kiss her one last time.

She fully expected to die. She was too cold to stay alive.

But after another minute she could see a faint light somewhere up ahead, filtering through snow and ice. She blinked, pretty much the only movement she was capable of at this stage. Her lungs burned. She held her head still to combat the dizziness.

Then his hands broke through, and fresh air rushed into their small tunnel. She coughed and watched as he climbed forward, careful enough not to kick snow into her face. She registered that he'd made it out, but didn't have the strength to go after him. Then he was back, head first, digging madly again, and her hands were enfolded in his strong grip at last as he pulled her to the surface.

Air.

Her lungs hurt and made squeaky noises as she breathed in. Her body was one solid block of ice.

The sun was blinding with the clouds gone, its brilliant rays reflecting off the snow. They hadn't had sun goggles in the first place; there'd been none on the pegs with the ski suits.

She couldn't keep her eyes open.

"Breathe." Miklos was holding her face

between his ungloved hands, rubbing her cheeks. His palms were the only warm things in a world of frozen snow. "Breathe."

She did her best.

"I'm sorry," he said after her wheezing quieted. He didn't let her go. "If it wasn't for me, you wouldn't be here."

She wanted to tell him that he didn't order the kidnapping, nor did he cause the avalanche, but her lungs still felt too tight to speak. He grabbed for her hand, and she winced when his touch brought more pain.

He was opening his ski suit the next moment, then pulled her gloves off, took her hands gently and pulled them under his clothes, pressing them against his bare skin.

Her body and senses were mostly numb. All she could feel was the warmth of his chest and the steady, reassuring beat of his heart. Thump, thump, thump. It gave her something to focus on other than the strange sleepiness that wrapped her brain in cotton.

Minutes passed before feeling returned to her hands.

"Can you walk?" he asked after a while.

She wanted more rest, to sleep for just a few seconds, but knew that way lay trouble. So she sat up, let him help her to her feet but immediately sunk to midcalf in the loose snow, like he had. And she realized that their skis were somewhere in the cave below.

Along with the gun, their only protection from whoever would be following. She didn't think the men who had kidnapped them were just going to let them go. And they were out in the open.

They scrambled off the top of the fresh snow, onto a path that was frozen solid, supporting their weight and making progress easier. He was there to prop her up every time she slipped.

Her mind still wasn't functioning all that clearly, so it took her a while to notice that instead of the direction they'd been following earlier, they were now headed straight down the mountain.

"Where are we going?"

"To the village," he said.

She blinked. The village he'd talked about earlier? Where, according to him, all kinds of danger awaited?

WHEN SHE COULD NO LONGER WALK, Miklos lifted her onto his back. She weighed next to nothing.

She didn't blame him once for being in this situation, didn't once complain. She just hung on to his shoulders with grim determination—after that initial, embarrassed protest.

The day was nearly over. They'd marched miles without food or water. She had wanted to eat snow, but he hadn't let her. That brought down a person's core temperature faster than anything.

"How are you holding up?" he asked.

She didn't respond. She hadn't responded to anything he'd asked in the last hour or so. She was completely still, no longer even shivering.

He figured the village to be about a mile ahead.

She needed serious medical help without delay. He pushed himself to the limit, knowing that every second counted.

When he heard voices from around a boulder, he slowly lowered Judi into the snow, noting her colorless face and barely blinking eyes, and dropped to his stomach next to her.

People were talking ahead. *Friend or foe?* was the topmost question in his mind.

Then the men came into view, wearing snowshoes, walking by at a distance of ten or fifteen meters, not yet noticing them. Their rifles threw long shadows in the twilight.

Chapter Five

The two men had guns. Miklos was alone, exhausted and unarmed. But as a soldier, he was prepared to take on odds like that or worse.

"Don't move. I'll be back." He barely breathed the words into Judi's ear, then rolled away from her and stole closer to the men on the uneven ground, moving between snow drifts. He hoped to catch what they were talking about, but by the time he got close enough, they seemed to be discussing nothing more interesting than the weather.

"Avalanche warning's out."

"Good reason not to be on the damn

mountain." The man stomped his feet. "Hope we won't be stuck up here long. Hate this damn cold." He stomped again.

Miklos noted the military-issue riffles. They weren't hunters. But they weren't military, either. No uniforms. They wore civilian clothing, coats large enough so they could hide their weapons if needed.

His first instinct was to take them on and take them down. He could gain weapons and possibly information from them. He was moving up to a crouch, getting ready to leap, but then ended up staying where he was, in cover.

This was not a military exercise or a routine mission.

If the slightest thing went wrong, if he were injured in any way, if they captured him—that would leave Judi in the cover of a snowbank somewhere behind him. Alone in the freezing cold. And she couldn't take these conditions much longer.

Frustration had him grinding his teeth as he stayed down and waited until the men moved on and eventually disappeared behind a boulder. He noted the direction they went and made sure to get a good look at their faces, the most he could do under the circumstances. Not nearly enough.

"Almost there," he whispered when he got back to Judi. He lifted her into his arms and, keeping his eyes open for more of the enemy, continued down the mountain. He pushed himself to the limit, aware that the men in the cabin had been talking about two days. Since then, one had passed.

Whatever the bastards were planning, he had less than twenty-four hours to stop them.

Any attacks would be happening today. At Maltmore Castle. The security measure of moving the family there had apparently been planned for by their enemies.

Unease crept up his spine. The enemy had gotten into the guarded section of the catacombs and had killed two guards. The enemy knew the emergency procedures for a security breach at the palace. Did they have inside help?

He had to reach his brothers and warn them. He had to reach General Rossi and ask him to send immediate help. And he had to get Judi to safety.

Even in a ski suit and boots she weighed little in his arms. His mood darkened a notch every time he looked at her pale cheeks and closed eyes. Snow had frozen to the tips of her eyelashes. He dipped his head and pressed his mouth against one eyelid, then the other, to warm them.

She looked like a princess under some

curse from the evil Snow Queen of fairy tales. And he was the prince. He was the one who was supposed to save her. He pushed harder, held her tighter. "Come on. Just a little longer. We're almost there."

The village came into view after the next bend, and he moved off the path, tracking through the snow toward the last row of houses, then weaving his way up the back alleys until he reached the kitchen entrance of the inn. "Hang on."

He knew the cook. Luigi had been a kitchen hand at the palace for a while until he'd decided to strike out on his own and make his dream of an Alpine inn a reality.

The heat of the kitchen, when he eased in, was such a sharp contrast to the outside weather that it stung his frozen cheeks.

Since Luigi was deaf, he could not call out to get his attention, nor would he have done so anyway. He needed to keep their arrival secret. The man felt the small vibration of the door opening and looked back, wide-eyed surprise on his round face. He was about to clap his hands to alert the kitchen staff to the prince's presence, but Miklos signaled for silence. Then mouthed a single word: *help.*

Luigi took in the woman in Miklos's arms and seemed to understand immediately. He had always been a champion at assessing situations at a glance and reading body language. He gestured behind a rack of cooling bread, and Miklos saw a narrow passageway that led to an equally narrow stone stairway. Miklos slipped in there, and Luigi came quickly after him. The man pointed and directed them until they were up the stairs, down the hall and inside a fairly spacious suite, all natural wood and animal furs and antlers, pictures of the mountains on the walls—an Alpine haven. Probably Luigi's quarters.

"Hypothermia." Miklos turned toward the man after he'd laid Judi on the bed. "I need a doctor you would trust with your life. With mine." He made sure to speak slowly and form the words with care.

Luigi couldn't hear, but he could read lips like nobody's business. He was already bringing blankets from the wooden chest at the foot of the bed, his large frame moving lightning fast. He nodded.

"Call him here. Don't say what it's for. Say there's been an accident in the kitchen. Nobody can know that we're at the inn."

Luigi was looking him over. "Okay?" he signaled.

And Miklos realized that he'd probably heard about the kidnapping on the news by now. Probably everyone had. Which meant he would have to cover his face when he ventured outside. "I'm fine. She's the one who needs help."

Luigi went out, then popped back in with a radio transmitter before leaving again. No phones up here. Miklos called in a message to the general on one of the military monitored frequencies. He passed on his current location and requested men to be dispatched to Maltmore Castle at once. He also asked the general to warn the princes immediately. Should anything happen, his brothers should be prepared.

By the time he was finished, Luigi was coming back with a steaming pot of tea and lamb stew seasoned with herbs. He barely handed over the tray before rushing off again. Miklos locked the door behind him.

He quickly removed his boots and ski suit,

then started on Judi's. "I'm going to get you warm. You're safe now. Open your eyes."

He discarded the boots and socks and took her slim feet into his hands. He warmed them slowly, without rubbing. If ice crystals had formed in her blood and cells, rubbing would only do more damage.

When some color returned to her skin, a good sign of blood moving to the extremities, no frostbite after all, he moved higher on her calves and massaged those to get the blood moving faster. He could only go so far before he had to remove her ski suit.

"I'm going to take this off to make you more comfortable."

She showed no sign that she heard him.

Worry ate at him, and anger that he'd gotten her into this. Fury built for the men who brought danger to his homeland, a peaceful country he loved more than life itself. Time was ticking. He would see to it that she was safe and in the care of the doctor. Then he'd go to his brothers.

She had his military jacket under the ski suit, then that flimsy spring dress she'd arrived in. He removed everything save her underwear, shrugged out of his own clothes, then climbed into bed with her, piling the blankets on top of them.

A hot bath would have helped, too, but that had to wait until she was conscious.

"You need heat. I'm not trying to seduce you." Then he added, out of habit, "Yet."

She was like a block of ice in his arms—albeit carved with perfect curves—but he was too worried about her to be distracted by them just now. He rubbed her arms, her back, pressed his cheeks to hers. Minutes passed, and she didn't seem to warm at all.

"Come on," he whispered into her ear and rubbed her velvety skin, close to the edge of desperation. "Wake up. We made it. You're safe."

That last bit was somewhat of an exaggeration, but he thought she could use hearing something positive. She didn't stir.

Maybe another approach would work better.

"Have I mentioned that we have practically no clothes on? I'm taking liberties with you here. It's time to start yelling."

Her eyes fluttered but didn't open. He needed to raise the stakes.

He pressed his cheek against hers again and whispered into her ear, "If you don't tell me to stop, I'm going to kiss you again."

"You're giving me whisker burns," she said weakly. "Get off."

He pulled back and looked into her eyes, which were blinking to gain focus. Her cheek did look a little reddened where he had rested his own against it. He ran his fingers over his cheeks. Rough. But shaving was the least of his worries.

"How are you feeling?"

"Like I've been buried by an avalanche." She flashed him a *duh* look, coming to life rapidly. "I'm perfectly fine. I just needed to warm up and rest a little."

Encouraging. Looked as if she was getting her spirit back.

"Can you move everything? Does anything hurt?"

She pulled away from him, wiggled around then looked under the blankets. "Why am I naked?" She did sound quite a bit stronger.

"We had to snuggle for heat." He was regretting how brief that part had been.

Her lavender eyes narrowed, her face flushed

with outrage. "You took advantage of me while I was unconscious?" That was the old Judi. Wide awake and ready to charge at him.

Gratitude hit him at first. They were safe. They were at the inn. She didn't seem to have suffered permanent damage. But that overwhelming sense of relief lasted only seconds before awareness sharpened that they were in bed together, *practically* naked.

They could fight.

Or they could…

He pulled her to him and rolled her under him in one smooth move, pinning her to the mattress. They were nose to nose. He needed to feel her that close, closer. He needed every inch of their bodies touching to know that she was safe and with him. "I haven't taken anything yet."

Enough heat filled his body all of a sudden to keep the both of them warm in a snowbank.

He caught a flicker of response in her eyes, but she said with forced severity, "You promised you wouldn't kiss me again."

"I won't. I'm thinking this time you'll kiss me." His gaze slipped to her lips that still didn't have their full color back.

Clearly they needed help.

"Why should I?" She shifted under him, maybe to push him off, maybe to get more comfortable, but the end result was that now they were perfectly aligned, hip to hip, his legs between hers.

"You're very grateful that I saved your life." He wished he could have come up with something snappier and brilliant instead, but his mind was too filled with Judi's nearness to think.

He could have lost her. They both could have been lost. Primal instinct pushed him to celebrate life in the most basic way.

He ran a hand up her side, caressing her smooth skin. Her full breasts pressed into his chest.

"It's basic first aid." He bent to nuzzle the sweet curve of her neck. "We have to get our blood moving."

"That's the most pitiful pickup line I ever heard." Her breath caught on the last word.

His hand stole up her ribcage, stopped just under her breast. "Kiss me because you want me."

The look she flashed him was seeped in denial. She wasn't going to make this easy. He should have known that. She hadn't made anything easy from the second she had gotten off the plane.

But need and urgency built between them. She had to feel it, too.

He gave up the game and lined up their lips, leaving only a hairsbreadth between them. "Kiss me because I want you. You're driving me crazy."

Her eyes went wide at his admission. Then the lids drifted down as she closed the negligible distance between them.

Her lips were soft and warming to his quickly. She initiated the kiss, and he didn't need any invitation beyond that. He tasted her, nibbling at the corner of her mouth, sweeping inside when at last she opened for him.

He wanted her. He'd told her the truth. But it shocked him just how much he wanted her. Even if she didn't want to marry him, even if she might not make the perfect princess. The thought stopped him. He had to marry the perfect princess—whoever could do the most good for his country. That was his duty. If after all this, Judi turned out not to be the right person for the job...

Thinking of duty seemed impossible with

Judi in his arms. He registered the danger in that, but plowed ahead nevertheless.

Her palms came to rest against his chest. Their legs were entwined under the covers as he drank from her. He shifted, making them both more comfortable, his hands moving up to cover her breast at last. She arched into his palm. A groan of pleasure bubbled up in his throat.

She was undoing him with unprecedented ease.

Her body was perfect, made for his. He was hard and ready between her legs, the adrenaline of escaping down the mountain still pulsing through his veins, rapidly turning to raging lust.

And she had such a tender look in her eyes.

He caught himself on the edge of madness, inched back from the ledge, dropped to his back next to her on the mattress.

He wasn't used to tenderness. He'd had lovers, and there'd been sex. But he was always aware that they were with him because they wanted something either his wealth or title could give them.

If Judi could have her way, she'd be running the opposite direction from him. The one woman he'd offered marriage to, and she'd turned him down without asking for a second to consider.

She ran a light hand over his shoulder. There was that tenderness again.

He knew how to handle lust. He didn't know what to do with this strange rapport or connection or whatever seemed to have grown between them.

"You should have something to eat and drink," he said toward the ceiling, not trusting himself to look at her passion-flushed face.

His body demanded that they finish what they'd started. His fingertips ached for the feel of her velvety skin. His mouth was parched for the taste of her. He could almost feel what it would be like to slide into her tight heat, to kiss her neck when she threw her head back in surrender, to swallow her moans as he made her his.

Control and sanity. He had to reach pretty deep inside to find any remnants of them, but in the end, he did. He waited while she collected herself and wrapped a blanket around her body, scrambled off the bed to the table and the food.

They probably should have gotten dressed, but he couldn't bring himself to give up the pleasure of watching her like this. When the doctor got here, he'd just tell her to undress anyway, so he could examine her.

The air around them vibrated with raw

need. The heat of their encounter left both of them shaken. Her auburn hair was mussed from his raking fingers. Her lips were swollen from his kisses. She wouldn't look at him.

"Where are we?" she asked after a minute, her voice still not one hundred percent steady.

"At the inn at the village of Vernesa."

"Have you called for help yet?"

"I radioed. Cell phones don't work up this high, and the place is too remote to be included in the telephone grid. The village doctor is on his way to check you out." He sat up and began to pull his clothes on. "We'll have the royal helicopter up here within the hour, with as many bodyguards as it can carry. You'll be safe. Just stay put in this room and rest until then."

Saying the words was beyond awkward, since what he'd been on the brink of doing with her was the opposite of rest. But she was definitely a woman who spoke her mind, so if she wanted to berate him for it, he was sure she would do just that.

So far, she hadn't.

He was starting to like her a lot more than he had ever expected. He'd been prepared to make the best of their marriage with or without mutual affection, had resolved to be the best husband to her that he was capable of being. The fact that he found himself enjoying her company was an unexpected bonus he was grateful for.

"You know, aside from the circumstances, I like spending time with you," he said as he dressed.

"We're not spending time together. We're running for our lives," she corrected with a peeved look.

And he liked that especially. That she never treated him like he was some three-eyed curiosity people stared at, or a prize to be won. From the first moment, he'd been just some crazy guy to her. He loved the novelty.

But he understood now that he'd taken the wrong approach with her back at the beginning. Considering the life she had lived until this point, of course she wouldn't be overjoyed with the idea of an arranged marriage.

"I'm sorry if I pushed. I mean before. And back there." He glanced at the bed. "I feel like I've always known you. I had the chancellor's reports and the pictures and the expectations that eventually…" He had no idea how to finish that without sounding inexcusably stupid.

"The expectation that we would eventually end up in bed?" She flashed him a droll look with one eyebrow sharply arched. But the flush in her cheeks told him that she wasn't entirely unaffected by the thought.

"I just mean—" What in hell did he mean? "I had a lot more time to get used to you, and the idea of the two of us together, than you did. And I tend to forget that."

She seemed to be waiting for something more from him.

It probably wasn't the admission that he still wanted her, even now, back in that bed, and not leaving it until at least spring thaw, which up here would be another month yet. Maybe Luigi could slide trays of food under the door.

If only they were two regular people, in regular times.

"Under different circumstances, maybe we could have dated," he offered.

"It wouldn't have been a date. It would have been an evaluation of my suitability. You're a prince."

He thought of the string of young ladies who were even now being "evaluated" for Arpad. She was right again.

And he was more than aware that he was still only half-dressed and she wasn't dressed at all, wrapped in a blanket. His body's response was predictable: heat, heat and more heat. He buttoned his pants and reached for his shirt, shrugged into it.

"At least I'm not a dodgy old prince," he said, more to himself than to her.

"Give it some time," she told him dryly.

He had half a mind to give her another way to occupy her smart mouth, but he enjoyed their verbal sparring as much as he enjoyed the physical connection between them. Almost as much.

Someone knocked before he could respond.

"Doctor's here," came a man's voice through the thick panel of wood.

Miklos was heading to the door when he happened to glance out the window and caught sight of a suspicious-looking man loitering opposite the inn's entrance, scanning people who were hurrying to get home for the night. The few people out in the biting wind rushed about their business, anxious to be back inside. This guy didn't seem to be heading anywhere. There was a noticeable bulge in his coat pocket.

He made a move like he was clearing his throat and adjusting his scarf, but Miklos could have sworn the guy was saying something into a radio behind his collar.

He fixed the guy's face in his mind and headed for the door. "I'll be off to get some weapons and check on something. You'll be in good hands with the doctor and Luigi," he said. "You're not to leave the inn without me. Under any circumstances," he added.

THE DOCTOR HAD GIVEN her a clean bill of health and told her to rest. Judi had slept, eaten pretty much all the food and drunk all the tea. Miklos still hadn't come back. The cuckoo clock on the wall showed four in the morning.

"Where are you?" she whispered to the window.

She brushed her index finger against her lips absentmindedly, then grew annoyed when she caught herself.

Yet she had to admit that his kisses had been amazing. And she couldn't deny that kissing him had very nearly turned into something more. He had the body of a soldier, all hard muscle and strength. And warmth. Oh, how she craved that heat that radiated from him. She could still smell the scent of his warm skin. She felt helpless against whatever drew her to him from the first moment, which was beyond disconcerting.

He was incredibly male, full of sex appeal, powerful in every sense of the word. But he could also be gentle. And he wasn't full of himself. He had a sense of humor. She had a feeling that if she didn't fight him tooth and nail, sooner or later the crazy attraction between them was going to do her in.

Dammit.

This was so not why she'd come to Valtria. Was it too much to ask to have some fun and celebrate her birthday without kidnappings and avalanches? Instead, here was Prince Miklos wanting all sorts of crazy and impossible things. Like a marriage of convenience, for heaven's sake. Well, for the country's sake, actually. And if she weren't careful, she could so easily fall in love with him—

Deep breath.

"That's not going to happen," she said to the empty room with some vehemence.

She'd been trying to take stock of her situation for the past hour and come to some kind of resolution. A small noise distracted her at the door, and when she looked expectantly to see whether it was Miklos or Luigi coming, she caught sight of the old-fashioned key jiggling in the lock then being pushed in.

Miklos and Luigi would knock if they wanted to come inside.

Something scraped against the door. The short hairs at the back of her neck stood up.

She moved quietly to the wardrobe. The blankets she'd been wrapped in were so warm and cozy that she'd been reluctant to give them up, but now she took the nearest pair of warm pants and a shirt, pulled them on, then shrugged into a pair of fur boots. They were too large, but she didn't have time to worry about that.

She grabbed a wool sweater next, but didn't waste time by putting it on immediately. She dashed to the window instead, climbed the writing desk in front of it, managing not to knock anything off, and opened the latch. The next second she was out on a narrow ledge with nowhere to go.

The cold air hit her face like a wall. She so did not want to go out in that again. And that was before she looked down.

Oh God.

The ground was farther away than she had expected. Cobblestones peeked from under slushy snow. Didn't look like a soft place to fall.

She pulled the window closed as much as she could behind her, teetering on the narrow ledge.

The lock in the door scraped again.

No time to hesitate.

A flagpole protruded from the stone wall about two feet to her left. She stepped on that to be out of sight of the window, and prayed that it would hold her weight. She wished she had known that she would be required to do some high-wire act on a flimsy perch *before* she had scarfed down Luigi's fabulous food.

She considered her situation, holding her breath. The ground was too far to jump to, the roof too high to reach. She was pretty much at the end of the road.

Where was Miklos when she needed him?

Voices filtered from the neighboring room on her other side.

"It couldn't have been Prince Miklos. He's not on a ski holiday, for heaven's sake. He was kidnapped," a man said, sounding like he was getting tired of the argument.

"I just know it was him. I only saw his

back when he turned down the stairs, but I'd recognize that back," a woman insisted.

The man groaned.

And Judi very nearly did, too. Next thing they knew, the media would be here before the rescue team, breathing down their necks.

She could hear the door in her room open then close, and that drew her attention from the bickering couple. She was hanging on to the uneven stones, holding the sweater with her teeth, quietly freezing to death once again. She hadn't had time to grab her gloves.

It was only a matter of time before whoever was inside the room would realize that the window was open a crack and would look out and spot her.

So when a canvas-top truck pulled up in front of the restaurant, Judi offered a brief prayer toward the snow clouds in the sky. Other than the truck, the street was deserted. She waited until the driver went inside, then jumped.

And got the wind knocked right out of her. Hitting the top of the truck felt pretty close to what it would have been like to hit the sidewalk. Apparently, she'd miscalculated.

Crates had been packed from top to bottom in the van. Hard, wooden crates that had no give in them whatsoever. She lay there for a minute, her hip and shoulders pulsing with pain, wishing she'd thought a little more before she'd leaped. Canvas-top jumps always worked out fine in the movies.

"Morgen habe ich wieder Freizeit," someone coming from a side alley said in German.

"Das weiss ich nicht..." another man responded as they walked out of hearing distance.

She didn't have much time to contemplate,

so she ran through her options as she pulled on the sweater then painfully climbed down and thumped into the snow on the street. For a second, she leaned against the van's side, against the sign that advertised Fresh Breads of Sacorata, and gasped to catch her breath. Sacorata was the next bigger town, according to Miklos, fifty miles into the valley.

She could stay and trust his protection. Except that he had his family to worry about. She would be nothing but an added handicap, slowing him down, putting him into even more danger.

Or she could get out of town on her own, out of the country before anyone realized that she was gone. She shouldn't have come to Valtria in the first place, that much was becoming increasingly clear.

Regardless of the fact that she was attracted to Miklos. More than attracted. She had nearly made love with him, might have if he hadn't pulled back.

She kissed him, when she had sworn she wouldn't. She was losing all good judgment. If she stayed with him, he'd somehow talk her into going along with the whole arranged-marriage insanity. She would have been willing to give him her body, just minutes ago, after having known him for only days. And he wanted so much more than that. He wanted her to honor some archaic agreement and become his wife, a princess.

Basically, he wanted her entire life. She would have to give up everything that was familiar to her, everything she had achieved so far. She couldn't do that. She thought of the gilded prison her life had been before her father's death. Receptions and protocols, never a moment allowed to let her guard down. Her family represented Valtria in a foreign land. And if that wasn't bad enough, there'd been that…

She didn't even want to think about the political enemy her father had unwittingly made, the one who'd begun a nasty media war against them, not sparing any member of the family. And since her stepmother decided to run for local office after her father's death, the spotlight had remained on them. Judi had grown up hating public life with a vengeance.

If she stayed in Valtria and let the prince work his magic on her, if he kissed her a few more times…She had a feeling that if she didn't leave right now, it'd be all over save for the wedding bells.

Best thing to do was to go with her screaming instinct of self-preservation.

She had to get out of Valtria before she did

something foolish like fall for the prince. She had to get out of the village before whoever had broken into the room upstairs came out and discovered her.

The van's driver was coming through the front door, a burly looking young man, although that could be just the down coat he wore against the cold. Judi wished she had something like that.

She approached him carefully, ready to turn tail and run at the first indication of trouble, aware that he could be allied with the men who pursued them. "Hi, are you going back to Sacorata?"

The young man's handsome face split into a grin, innocent pleasure that could not be faked. "I should be. This is my only delivery up here. But I can stay if you wish," he said with a slight accent and stepped closer, his gaze warm on her face, a playful glint in his eyes.

"Actually, I was hoping for a ride." She gave him a look that said pretty please. She was shivering inside. She should have grabbed a coat before she left the inn.

His smile widened. "Are you visiting up here? Do you have any ski gear?" He glanced toward the inn. "I can help you bring it out. There's not much room in the back, but we can probably squeeze your gear in."

She could hear voices from inside the entryway. Somebody would be coming out in a second. Could be the same men who were after her and the prince.

"I could show you some of the best slopes in a couple of hours. I'm pretty good at skiing. I could even show you some slopes that are private."

God help her, the driver was actually flirting.

She stepped to the cab and opened the door. "Just meeting up with some girlfriends in town for breakfast. I'll tell you everything along the way."

Miklos was so going to kill her for doing this. He was going to be mad beyond belief. Probably not many women had ever run from the prince, especially not ones he had explicit plans for. He was going to be royally angry.

Not that they needed to ever meet again.

He would be busy saving Valtria, and she would be at a safe distance in D.C. Why didn't the thought of that fill her with relief?

"Early risers, eh?"

"Want to hit the slopes as soon as they open." She made up the story as she got in.

She flattened herself against the back of the seat and turned her head toward the driver's side to hide her profile form the men who were coming from the inn. The warmth of the cab felt great.

Go, go, go.

She didn't dare turn to steal a peek at whoever was leaving the inn.

"My name is Gunther," the young man said as he slipped into his seat and slammed the door behind him.

Miklos would be worried about her. She would try to get a message to him somehow from the airport. He'd mentioned that he had radio contact with a man named General Rossi. Maybe through him.

"Judi. How long does it take to get to Sacorata from here?"

"Two hours at least."

"Oh dear. I'd hate to be late." She made an apologetic face. "Do you think we could hurry?"

Twenty minutes of Gunther's outrageous flirting later, they'd left the village behind and were swerving over the ice-covered roads.

She hung on for dear life and regretted having said anything. Gunther was using speed and reckless driving to try to impress her.

Which turned out not to be the biggest problem she faced, even if she'd been seriously beginning to fear loss of life or limb. An hour out of the village, she spotted a roadblock up ahead, armed men waiting, at least a half-dozen ominous dark figures in the moonlit landscape, big and menacing.

"Stop!" She grabbed Gunther's arm.

But Gunther didn't understand how much trouble they were in and didn't slow the truck until it was too late. By then, the armed men had noticed them and were moving in for the kill.

Chapter Six

She'd been taken.

Anger and concern about ripped him apart as Miklos paced the room, scanning it for clues, willing her to come walking back in, knowing he waited for that in vain. She wouldn't have left without her gloves and at least a parka if she'd left on her own, willingly.

She was out there, the captive of conscienceless bastards somewhere in the cold, barely dressed, when what she needed was warmth and rest.

And him.

She needed him by her side, damn it all.

He cursed himself for leaving her. He'd thought he would be back before the doctor left. But the suspicious man in front of the inn had been gone by the time Miklos made his way down to the street, so he had to do a quick sweep of the village to find the guy. He did, a few streets down. By then the man had two other thugs with him. He followed them, then spent precious hours staking out the derelict cabin at the edge of town where they led him. Men coming and going was all he'd seen, watching and waiting all night, gaining little information beyond the obvious: the enemy was numerous and well armed with military-issue weapons.

He'd gained nothing and lost Judi in the bargain. And could have lost Luigi, too. Miklos glanced at the man who was sitting in an old-fashioned armchair, rubbing the back of his head, stopping long enough to half sign, half say, "I'm sorry. I never saw them coming."

"Not your fault," Miklos told him. "Do you need a doctor?" He nodded toward the bump above the man's nape.

Luigi shook his head.

Where in hell was the rescue team he'd asked for? They should have been here long ago. Maybe something was going down that he didn't know about, something that suddenly required the general's full attention and temporarily diverted the chopper the man must have sent here.

"General Rossi should have alerted the royal guard by now. The helicopter is on its way with at least a dozen men." He'd also asked the general to dispatch a military unit to protect Maltmore Castle. They might be there already.

"So the only vehicle that left the inn today went to Sacorata?" he asked again.

Luigi nodded.

"I'm going after her." General Rossi was going to blow a fuse, but he would deal with the man later. "Thanks for the help. Take care of yourself," he said as he reached for the small, handheld radio that Luigi had scared up for him.

A snowmobile waited in the alley behind the inn, also courtesy of Luigi. Miklos drove south on the winding road, looking for any meaningful tracks. The sun was taking its time coming up, darkness lingering late this time of the year. But he could make out the tracks of vans, with snow chains on the tires, and snowmobiles that had crisscrossed the road.

Judi could be anywhere by now.

Miklos gripped the handlebars tight enough to break them. The dawn air was brisk, the cold nipping at his face, wind pushing against him. He was all alone in the vast landscape.

Snow stretched for miles and miles, but farther south he could see green-capped hills. He floored the snowmobile, nearly wiping out a while later when he spotted a jumble of footprints and tried to stop too fast.

A group of people had trampled the snowbank; vehicles had parked by the side of the road. Vehicles that hadn't gone to Sacorata, but driven off on the top of the frozen snow toward the east instead. He was grateful for Luigi's snowmobile that allowed him to easily follow the tracks.

In the back of his mind, he was aware that this could be a trap. Whoever had taken Judi could have taken her specifically to draw him out. There had been no attempt made to cover their tracks. They might as well have drawn him a map.

The smart thing would have been to wait for the general's men. He radioed in his new position, and found the general had been waiting for him on the other end.

"We've been trying to reach you. The chopper that was taking the royal guards to you had some technical problems and had to make an emergency landing. I've sent another with my own men. I apologize for the delay, Your Highness." He paused. "Chancellor Hansen has been placed under house arrest," the general informed him.

"He can't have anything to do with this." Denial sprang to his lips at once.

He knew the chancellor too well to ever question his loyalties. They didn't have time to go down the wrong path. Not now, not when so many lives were on the line, people who were so important to him.

"He alone had been left behind when you and the future princess were taken. Unharmed." The general emphasized the last word. "And we've discovered some communications."

Which were probably nothing, but the general tended to be overprotective of the royal family, particularly Miklos, who was like another son to him. Especially since the man didn't always see eye to eye with his own son, who'd refused a military career. But with the other princes, too, he'd always been on friendly terms, always there to offer advice or support. In fact, at times the queen had wondered out loud if there didn't exist a rivalry for the princes' affection between the chancellor and the general.

Maybe the rivalry between them had pre-judiced them against each other.

"It couldn't be Chancellor Hansen," Miklos insisted, keeping his eyes on where he was going. He couldn't afford to drive into a ditch and flip the snowmobile over.

"He's been maintaining contact with the top man of the Freedom Council over the last three months," the general said gravely.

That had the power of turning Miklos's blood a few degrees colder. They didn't even know the identities of the three men who led the Council, other than that they were powerful businessmen. Funding for the Council was never in short supply.

A sharp sense of betrayal cut through him and stole the breath from his lungs. The chancellor had been like a surrogate father to the princes.

"Just hold him. Don't do anything else until I get there," he told the man who outranked him in the army but owed his fealty to him as prince. "The Queen?"

"Doing well. At the last report."

"My brothers?"

"Locked up tight at Maltmore Castle and

protected by the royal guard. I sent a full platoon of reinforcements to secure the perimeter. Hold your position and stay out of sight. Your backup is on its way."

He let the general know in which direction he was heading and plowed ahead into the approaching night.

THE MEN SWITCHED BETWEEN German and Hungarian. Judi didn't speak enough of either to understand, although, at Aunt Viola's urging, she'd taken lessons as part of staying in touch with her parents' heritage.

Had she known that her life would one day come to depend on her vocabulary, she would have paid more careful attention in class.

She was alone, tied up in a small cave, straining to listen for any sound beyond the men who were talking outside the cave's entrance. She could think of little else but Gunther as they cut him down without mercy. His only sin had been giving her a ride.

Tears stung her eyes at the memory.

His cold-blooded murder had drained her strength. She had allowed herself to be captured, but was beginning to wonder now if she wouldn't have been better off fighting, no matter what they would have done to her.

A distant rumble drew her from her dark thoughts. She turned her head to hear better. Couldn't catch it again. Maybe she'd imagined the sound.

Or maybe not. Here it came again.

And all of a sudden her nerve endings buzzed with anxiety. As if a switch had been flipped in her brain, she could think of little else than being trapped in her cold prison by another avalanche. She could feel the panic and the cold of their mad dig, knew she would have never made it to the surface without Miklos.

She felt as if she were suffocating all over again.

Breathe slow.

Breathe deep.

Her captors said Miklos's name enough times for her to know that she was nothing but bait in a trap. What they didn't understand was that Miklos wouldn't come for her. Duty to his country and the monarchy were the very spine of the man. Warning his brothers would be his first priority. He was probably on his way to Maltmore Castle already.

And she didn't blame him one bit. She had no siblings, her family long gone, but she was sure she would have done the same in his position. As much as she resented it at the beginning, along the way she had come to like and respect his old-fashioned sense of honor.

He was a man like no other.

A cliché, but so true in this case. He was a man of principle, of strong character. If things were different, if they'd met under different circumstances…The memory of his kisses distracted her from her fears for a minute.

When they had first been captured, faced with overwhelming force and tied up in a cabin in the mountains, she would have given up and would have done little but await her fate if Miklos hadn't been there. But he'd taught her to fight against impossible odds. He'd gotten them out of the cabin, gotten them out of the cave after the avalanche. He'd never given up. And she wasn't going to give up, either.

She yanked at the ropes behind her back, then felt along the rock wall for a sharp protrusion. When she found it, she rubbed the rope against it. She had to save herself.

Miklos couldn't save her this time. He had to save his country. And as much as she wished that he were with her, she knew he was doing the right thing.

She said a brief prayer that he would make it safely to Maltmore Castle. The fate of the royal family had great bearing on the fate of the country. And when she thought of all those women and children and everyone who lived in and loved this small country, those millions of Valtrian lives, her own didn't seem all that important in comparison.

She was starting to understand Miklos's sense of duty.

She worked on the rope, but with little success. Maybe the rock wasn't sharp enough, or maybe she was too tired to provide enough pressure. She took a moment to rest, then tried again, aware that she didn't have too many more lives left and they were at level ten of the game.

HE HAD THE CAVE IN sight, but he was out-numbered at least twenty to one. Could be more. The cave might hold others. Miklos lay on his stomach and mapped the area: three military trucks and a tank.

The men back in the village had military-issue weapons. A picture started to form, even though he hated to consider that a group of soldiers from the Valtrian Army could be turned against the monarchy they'd sworn to protect.

He couldn't not think about the fact that the chancellor's youngest brother was an army colonel. The sense of betrayal that washed over him was a distraction he couldn't afford. He'd deal with the chancellor's role in all this later.

The presence of the tank and the location of the cave should have been passed along to General Rossi, as well as Miklos's suspicions about traitors in their ranks. But now that he saw the military equipment here, he couldn't be sure that his enemies wouldn't pick up his transmission with their own radios. They'd definitely be monitoring the military channels.

The general knew which way Miklos had been heading, and he was a military man; being ready for anything and everything was his basic stance. They would find him. And when they did, the chopper had enough fire-power to take care of the tank.

The fact that for a second he considered whether the general might not have turned against him, too, just showed how exhausted he was. The general had always treated him like a son. He needed to snap out of paranoia before he made things worse than they were.

Backup couldn't be that far away.

At least the sun was finally up, so he had no trouble with visibility.

Miklos moved ahead and identified four men standing guard at the perimeter of the enemy camp, at a distance from the others. None were in an easily approachable position. He stole toward the one closest to him. The man was leaning against a large rock, his back protected. Flat, snowy ground lay between him and Miklos, not much to hide behind if Miklos tried to approach him.

Miklos dropped to his stomach and crawled forward as far as he dared, waited for the man to look the other way, then rose enough to give his arm free range to move as he threw one of Luigi's knives. He'd armed himself as best he could before taking off after Judi, but a couple of kitchen knives seemed pitiful compared to the enemy's arsenal.

The knife hit where he'd aimed it, went through the man's throat, preventing a shout. Miklos was moving forward even as the man folded to the ground. He ignored the hands that clawed at the bloody throat, as the man choked on his own blood, and finished the job without wasting time. He grabbed the man's communications unit and his weapon, kicked enough snow over the prone figure so that he wouldn't be immediately visible if one of his buddies came this way. His mouth thinned as he retrieved his weapon and registered how young the guy was, no more than midtwenties. He covered up the face. He had no sympathy for traitors.

He moved along the rock that formed the top of the cave. The general had only sent a platoon to Maltmore, thirty soldiers. He didn't realize that the army had been compromised, that their enemies had tanks. And if they had this one, they could have others. On their way to Maltmore Castle or already there. The clock was ticking.

Miklos climbed the rock and stole forward until he was above the next guard. He took off his belt quietly, held the ends and in a sudden movement looped it and positioned it so that it caught the man under the chin. Then he pulled up as hard as he could, hard enough to pull the man's body off the ground and up to the top of the rock, to him. The man kicked wildly, then less and less as he suffocated. Miklos dragged the body behind a pile of snow on top of the rock and left it there.

He glanced at the sky, hoping for the chopper, but all he could see was more snow clouds gathering. Judi was in the cave, he was pretty sure of that. Inside the cave and at the mercy of whoever held her.

The third guard was relieving himself when Miklos snuck up behind him. He broke the man's neck in one smooth move, killing the traitor. Miklos moved along, ready for the next.

His education as a prince might have told him that these were his subjects, men he was supposed to protect, but his military training was stronger just now. They were the enemy. They sought to destroy the country and his family.

They'd taken Judi. He couldn't find it in himself to forgive.

The fourth guard caught sight of him coming. He lifted his rifle, but was too slow, couldn't get off a shot before Miklos vaulted over the distance between them and brought him down with enough force to smash the guy's skull on the rocks on the ground. He pulled the man behind a bush, collected his ammunition and hand grenade then stole closer to the cave.

He could count only sixteen of the enemy now. Some had gone into the cave. He didn't want those bastards anywhere near her.

He was still outnumbered, but in addition to the small handgun and knives he'd picked up in the village, he also had a rifle now with plenty of ammunition, and four hand grenades. He positioned himself behind a boulder, pulled the pin from one of the grenades—he'd picked one off each man he'd taken out so far—and let it fly.

One of the trucks blew sky-high.

Smoke, fire and chaos reigned, his enemies pouring out of the cave. He shot at will and brought down four, ran to the cover of the next boulder once his location at the first was compromised, then tossed another grenade. This one missed, since the men were shooting blindly in every direction and he didn't have time to take careful aim. The explosion didn't take out the truck he'd targeted, but it did bring down three men who'd been running up to the vehicle.

A dozen or so of the enemy were left.

He didn't have time to congratulate himself. The next second, a bullet grazed his knee. He limped out of his hiding place, ducking more bullets, lunging behind a bigger rock that could provide more coverage. Bullets pinged off the rock. Then everything went quiet. And then another sound came that made the short hairs at the back of his neck rise.

He looked out for just one glimpse.

Damn. Damn. Damn. The tank was coming his way.

The next second, the top of the boulder he was hiding behind blew off, deafening him, shards of stone raining from above. The force of the explosion knocked him off his feet.

Where in hell was General Rossi?

No longer on the offensive, Miklos ran for his life now, ignoring the pain in his knee and the blood that was running into his left eye from a cut on his forehead.

He stopped long enough to toss another grenade behind him, and this time he lucked out even as his knee gave. The grenade went right in the top and when it blew it took out everyone and everything inside the tank.

Miklos dashed to the left, mowed down with his rifle the four men who were charging him head-on. He figured there were now only half a dozen left. Everything went quiet all of a sudden. And after a while, he realized that those who were still alive had retreated into the cave.

He couldn't shoot blindly, nor toss a grenade. Not with Judi in there.

She was the perfect hostage. The bastards probably knew that as long as they had her, he wasn't going to do anything. Unless something had happened to her already. He hadn't heard her voice once during the fight—the thought filled him with both dread and murderous rage.

He went around the entrance, flattened himself to the rock outside. The cave was too dark to see beyond the first dozen feet. Large and cavernous was his first impression, with plenty of rock formations for the bastards to hide behind.

He moved back, grabbed a fallen man and held the body in front of him as he approached the cave. He didn't get far before they shot at him anyway. The body caught the bullets, but would not make a dependable shield. He tossed it aside and dove behind the nearest big rock. At least he was now inside the cave.

"I am Prince Miklos of the House of Kerkay. You are committing an act of treason. Let the hostage go," he called out, pressing a hand to his bleeding knee.

Their only response was more bullets.

When they quieted, he popped up for a second, saw movement and shot blindly that way. The shout that rose told him that he had got his man. He kept down for the next minute or so as bullets pelted the rock he was hiding behind.

They were at an impasse. He couldn't move forward, and they couldn't get by him to get out of the cave.

Or could they?

"Miklos!" He heard Judi's plea the next second. "Don't shoot."

And when he popped up again, he saw her emerge from behind a dark rock formation, a man behind her, twisting her arm back, a gun to her head.

"Throw your weapons forward," the man said.

The cave was too dark to see whether she was hurt. But she was alive. She was well enough to stand. He found hope in that. But it wasn't time yet to give in to relief, to draw her into his arms and kiss her.

He badly wanted to, needed to kiss her again.

First he had to get them out of here. Miklos tossed the rifle and two of his knives. He kept his last knife and his last grenade hidden, tossed his handgun that was now out of bullets.

"Stand with your hands in the air."

Like hell. "Let her go. She has nothing to do with this. Let her go and take me."

"We already have you," the man sneered.

Miklos pulled the pin from his last grenade then rose, one hand in the air, the other holding the grenade to his chest, under his palm, invisible to the man. "I'm hit." Come on, move forward, move forward more.

"Both hands in the air!" the man snapped.

Sweat beaded on Miklos's forehead. If he made a sudden move to put the pin back in, he'd be shot. If he tossed the grenade now, he'd put Judi in more jeopardy.

But the man moved forward at last, switching his aim from Judi to Miklos. Four of his buddies rose up from behind the rock at his back. They stayed where they were, but kept their weapons trained on Miklos. When Judi and the bastard who held her got far enough from them to be out of harm's way, Miklos lunged forward, tossing the grenade at those men, letting his knife slide into his palm from his sleeve with the same movement, then throwing that at the one who held Judi.

The grenade hit, shaking the cave and sending rocks flying like deadly missiles through the air. The knife missed, the man ducking out of the way in the last second. He was on the ground, bowled over by the explosion, looking stunned. But he still had his riffle, and he still had Judi.

Miklos had nothing.

He couldn't do anything else but throw himself at the bastard.

His ears were ringing from the explosion in the closed confines of the cave. Long seconds passed as he desperately fought for the sole weapon within reach. Then a noise reached them from the outside: the rumble of a chopper.

Dust and more rocks rained on them from

above, and he realized that the cave's roof had been damaged enough that it could collapse. Even perhaps from the vibration the chopper was causing in the air.

"Get out of the cave!" he yelled toward Judi just as his enemy kicked him full force in his busted knee and made him see stars.

"I'm not leaving you." She had a large stone in her hands. She looked like some wild, Amazonian maiden, her auburn hair near black in the dark of the cave.

"Get out!"

She tried to bend to hit the bad guy, but they were rolling too fast, fighting too furiously for her to hit her target. Not that she didn't try. She dropped the stone when she realized it was as much a liability as it was a weapon. She tried to throw herself on the man's legs next, to help Miklos, but the bastard kicked at her, kicked hard enough so

she went bouncing off a boulder behind them.

The men rolled. Miklos didn't dare take his
attention off his opponent. A minute passed
before Judi limped back, and he could
breathe again.

"Go!" He ground out the single word as he
fought, aware that the cave could come down
on top of them at any second. "Get help."

He had both hands on the rifle, but the man
had his finger on the trigger. He squeezed, the
shots going wild, into the already perilous
ceiling. More shards flew from above.

In addition to the blood from the cut on his
forehead, Miklos also had dust in his eyes,
nearly blinding him. His knee throbbed with
a sharp pain and didn't support him when he
tried to flip his enemy. At least Judi was safe;
he clung to that thought. Judi would be safe,
whatever happened to him.

He had done all he could do. The general had already sent help and warning to the other princes. He groaned as the man slammed him against the rock floor. Then he heard Judi's voice outside, or at least he thought he did, and that gave him new strength. He brought his head hard against the man's chin and watched his head flop back.

The momentary surprise was enough to get the gun away from him. Miklos didn't hesitate to shoot, point-blank.

He barely took a second to catch his breath before he struggled to his feet and started limping toward the mouth of the cave. The royal helicopter hadn't come for them. The general had sent an Apache instead. His men were already on the ground, all around the copter.

He lowered his weapon.

Then he spotted Judi through the chopper's

open door, in the back. Tied and gagged, her eyes filled with tears. She struggled against her ropes, but wasn't getting anywhere.

Something was terribly wrong.

They'd been betrayed.

And he had way too little strength left in him. He had a sick feeling that this might be the end of the road for the both of them. But the look in her eyes wouldn't let him give in to pain and accept his fate.

He blinked the blood and dust from his eyes. "What in hell are you—" He charged forward, raising his gun, ready to keep going with the fight until his legs gave way from under him.

Which turned out to be right that second. He crashed to one knee on the snow-dotted rocks, pain shooting up his leg and momentarily knocking the air from his lungs.

"Judi!" He had to get to her. He crawled in the snow, managing another few feet, knowing that what he had left wasn't going to be enough.

He had failed.

He had underestimated the enemy and let down Judi, his family and his people. He should have known something wasn't right, caught some sign, should have sensed that something had been off with the general.

Hot fury burned through him. He had loved the man like a father. He had confided in him in the past, listened to his advice. He had thought the bastard a hero.

If the army was against the monarchy... No other force in the country was strong enough to stand against the Valtrian Army. The army he'd helped to make more efficient, helped to strengthen. The very one he served in.

With so many of his friends, men he considered brothers.

Would they, too, fight against him?

He looked up at Judi, wanting to make her understand, somehow, how sorry he was that he wasn't going to be able to save her. He would have given anything to see her safe, but the men who'd captured them had no reason to bargain.

Chapter Seven

The last time Miklos had been to the compound, as a guest, General Rossi had called it his mountain hunting hideaway. Since then, the place had taken on the character of a miniature military base, crammed with army trucks and the odd tank or two, soldiers—*traitors*—filling the guesthouses.

Since they were both gagged, the best Miklos could manage was a slight brush against Judi's hands when they'd been pushed out of the chopper. He wanted to let her know that as long as he was alive, he was not going to let anything happen to her.

Which wasn't much of a guarantee under the circumstances.

"Move it." They were shoved forward, taken into a cement structure that looked like a military bunker, then down a flight of stairs.

Prison cells. When had the general put this in? How long had he been preparing? The sense of betrayal was a heavy weight that pushed him down, along with the blame he felt for not figuring this out earlier. He met with the general at least once a week. How many times had they talked just this month? If he'd caught even a hint that something had been off, he could have saved his family.

His hands fisted, but he could do nothing. The situation looked as dire as it possibly could. They faced overwhelming opposition forces. So he did what any good soldier would do under the circumstances: kept a sharp eye out for a small break, something he could turn to his advantage. And he refused to give up hope.

"Your new royal suite is waiting," one of the soldiers mocked, stepping between his prisoners.

Miklos could do little to reassure Judi when her panicked gaze flew to him.

But when they went inside and he spotted the two cells, almost like bear cages, he saw that only one was empty. Then, when he got used to the semidarkness, he recognized the other prisoner, despite the fact that the man's face was badly beaten and bloodied.

Miklos lurched toward the bars, bruising his shoulder when he broke free from the hold of the soldier behind him, and slammed against the inch-thick steel rods. The gag loosened from his mouth in the process. "Chancellor?"

But the man didn't move.

"Chancellor! It's Miklos." It seemed impossible now that he could have suspected the chancellor of turning against the monarchy, even for a second.

He had trusted the general implicitly because they were both military men. The chancellor was a politician through and through, embroiled in a number of intrigues at court in his younger years, most involving young ladies, then political ones later. And even though Miklos had been shocked when the general had accused him, in the back of his mind there had been that little doubt, the knowledge that the chancellor had a reputation for being a wheeler and dealer.

"Chancellor Hansen!" He started to look the man over for signs of how serious his injuries might be but was unceremoniously yanked away from the bars, then shoved into the empty cell with Judi.

One of the soldiers pulled a knife and cut their gags as well as the plastic ties that had held their hands together. Then the door swung shut with a creak and a bang. The lock turned.

At least they were together.

He wanted to take Judi into his arms, but the men were heading toward the other cell. He threw himself against the bars, from the inside this time.

"Chancellor Hansen," he shouted. Then as the soldiers opened the old man's cell, he called out an order. "Do not touch him!"

Only when they dragged the chancellor out, over the uneven, cold floor, did he realize that his old friend could no longer hear him, nor could he feel the soldiers' rough handling.

He blinked as the man's lifeless body was dragged out. Miklos beat against the bars until his hands turned bloody, hard rage filling him. Then he leaned against the cold wall of the cell, seeing little more than the chancellor's bloodied, lifeless body.

His muscles were rigid with grief, his soul black with the need for revenge. When he got out of here—and he would—those sons of... He was pure soldier in that moment, a fighting machine that could and would take his enemies apart with his bare hands.

Judi stepped up next to him. Just stood there within touching distance, waiting. Her presence made it impossible to fully settle into the darkness that tried to claim him, no matter how much he wanted to do just that.

"He was a man of peace." He bit out the words and felt broken, unable to erase the sight from his mind. A man of peace through and through. How could he have ever doubted it? "Hurting him was completely unnecessary. They had nothing to gain by killing him."

But they'd done it anyway. In cold blood. A kind old man, and they had beaten him to death. Rage was filling Miklos to the brim. He wanted to strike out at anything and everything.

"Were you close?" Judi put a hand on his shoulder. Her voice sounded weak with shock. She wasn't a soldier, wasn't used to seeing violence.

Hell, the past twenty-four hours were getting to be too much even for him. "As close as family." Bile burned his throat. He stepped away from her, his rage too strong, his emotions too tumultuous to be near anyone. He wanted to rip apart their cell brick by brick and go after the general.

She came to him, not understanding his need for space. When he was practically cornered, she leaned against him and wrapped her arms around his waist. "I'm sorry."

And to his surprise, he didn't feel like shaking off her touch. But still, his fury took time to cool. A few minutes passed before he rested his chin on the top of her head and could at least accept a small portion of the comfort she was offering.

Each breath he took brought her scent to him, making it impossible to ignore her.

He couldn't remember the last time anyone had tried to give him comfort. Maybe the nursemaids when he'd been little. His mother had always been too busy with matters of state to spend much time with her children. The extent of their contact was when the governesses brought the children in for her inspection for one full hour each day before dinner. His father believed in bringing up strong boys, toughening them up early for the roles they would have to play in life. For this he employed fencing and wrestling tutors. As far as personal time went, he did take them skiing once a year.

Judi hugged him tighter.

He didn't realize until then just how good a gentle touch could feel, that he could need something like that. But now that he had it, he didn't want to let it go. She was the one person outside his closest family who didn't want anything from him. In fact, all she wanted was to go home.

But for now she was still here. Still unharmed for the most. They were still together.

He closed his arms around her. "Are you warm enough?"

There was no heat in the dungeon, and all

she had on was a sweater. He had a good parka he'd gotten from Luigi.

He'd brought warm clothes for her, too, but he hadn't been able to get back to his snowmobile after the fight. He'd been too busy getting tied up and shoved up into the chopper.

"I'm fine."

Of course she was. She was as tough as any soldier he'd ever known, which he greatly admired about her. But that toughness should never have been tested like this. He pushed her back a little, opened his parka and settled her against his body before closing the parka on her back. He did his best to remain detached and keep his focus on the door as their bodies molded together.

"What's going to happen to us?" she asked and trembled against him slightly.

Probably the same thing that had happened to Chancellor Hansen, he thought, but couldn't say the words to her. "There are more people who are loyal to the monarchy than who are against us."

"So we'll be saved?"

He didn't count on that too much. Eventually, good would win over evil, he was sure of that. But he couldn't guarantee how fast that would happen, whether it would be too late for them. And his family. He would have given anything for news of his mother and brothers.

"Oh," she said after a while when he didn't answer. "Things are worse than you thought, aren't they?"

Still he hesitated to share his thoughts with her. But she was in the middle of the danger with him. She had a right to know.

"Like I told you, just before I left to receive you at the airport, I received intelligence that there was a plot against Arpad, the crown prince." He still couldn't say that without seeing red.

Her hold tightened around him. "And there you were, worried about your brother's life, having to deal with me."

He didn't mind dealing with her. He acknowledged the odd thought. She was worth any trouble. And he would defend her with his life if it came down to it.

"There's more, isn't there?" She tilted up her head.

"To go after Arpad, a small group of assassins would have been the most logical. Sneak in, sneak out. To remove Arpad, they didn't need to get the army involved, didn't need to lay siege to Maltmore Castle."

"They want the whole royal family." She finished the thought for him in a shaky voice, sounding as stunned as he felt by the prospect.

"Yes." The Freedom Council must have

decided that trying to make the royal family abdicate wasn't worth the effort. They didn't want a cumbersome public discourse that would take forever.

"I think our enemies might be engineering a revolution. A fake revolution. The people aren't the ones rising up, but that's what they'll say later. The Freedom Council somehow gained the general's support. The general turned the army or part of the army…" A prince didn't use foul language. But if he did, this would have been the perfect time to swear.

"Why not let you reach your brothers at Maltmore? He could have had the whole family taken out all at once. Wouldn't that make more sense than having you separately kidnapped?"

"I'm an army man. Some of the army might not go up against the castle if they think they're going up against me. The general can cook up some story about my family, about something terrible my brothers did or new taxes the monarchy is planning that would burden the common man, whatever. But a lot of the soldiers know me. The general might even say that my own brothers killed me because I stood up for the people. He plans on taking care of me separately."

He couldn't see much of her in the dim prison, but he could tell that she was staring at him with an expression of wide-eyed horror on her face.

"And the soldiers here? They saw you already. They know that the general kidnapped you. Why don't they turn against him and set you free?" she asked after a while.

"I haven't seen one yet that I know. They must have been brought in from outlying posts, maybe from the eastern border. No telling what lies they've been told. They are loyal to their general. We will not find any allies here."

But they had to break out somehow.

His brothers and mother were at Maltmore Castle, which had been surrounded by the general's men on pretense of protection. Had they made their move yet? Was his family already dead?

Judi laid her head against his chest, her voice a mere whisper when she spoke. "How much time do you think we have left?"

JUDI WAS LEANING AGAINST the wall as she sat next to Miklos, their shoulders touching. She needed that connection.

Their small prison had no bed, no table, no bucket. It looked more like a bear cage than a prison cell. They'd been dumped in here about an hour ago, but their captors clearly weren't planning on keeping them too long. She could figure that out on her own, even if Miklos had evaded her question earlier.

They had been left in the dark—the light that filtered in under the door was precious little—and it was cold. But at least the bunker was closed, and it kept the wind out. And being partially underground, it wasn't nearly as cold as that first cave up high on the mountain.

The thought sent a shiver through her body.

"Did they hurt you when they took you from the inn?" Miklos's voice cut the darkness and drew her from those frozen memories.

She'd seen him looking her over a couple of times on the way here in the chopper, checking for injuries. He must have seen the one bruise on her cheek. They'd done little beyond pushing her around. "I'm fine."

"You always say that," he told her as if he didn't fully believe her.

"They only needed me to get you to come to them. You should have stayed away."

He said nothing to that.

"They didn't exactly take me from the inn," she confessed. "They tried, I think. Someone was breaking in. But I climbed out the window."

She could feel as he shifted toward her. "We weren't on the first floor."

"I jumped on top of a truck."

Ominous silence stretched between them.

"Then I asked the driver to take me to Sacorata." It had been a good plan. It could have worked. If she could have gotten away, then he wouldn't have had to save her. He could be at Maltmore Castle by now, instead of keeping her company in some nasty dungeon.

More silence. She was beginning to think that wasn't good.

"I thought if I stayed, I'd just hold you back." He had to understand that.

"You got into a truck with a strange man?" His voice was deceptively controlled.

"He seemed nice." Okay, that did sound pretty stupid in hindsight, but at the time she hadn't had many options.

Yet more silence came from the prince.

"Having to worry about me was the last thing you needed." That was a fact he couldn't argue with. She hoped.

"And just how far did you plan to run?" His voice had an edge to it.

She bit her bottom lip. "Home?"

She could hear him breathing. His chest huffed like a bellows.

"You were leaving me for my own good," he stated flatly.

"Right." Why did she think that she wasn't doing a good job at convincing him?

"And then what happened?"

She shivered at the memory. "We ran into a roadblock a couple of miles out of town. They—" She swallowed. "They just shot the driver. He couldn't have been older than I am. All he was doing was helping me. They yanked me out of the cab, and then they shot him point-blank." Her voice broke.

All that blood in the cab. God.

Gunther had been killed because of her. Because she had begged a ride from him. The stress and danger of the last two days crashed down on her, along with the sure knowledge that Miklos and she would soon be joining Gunther wherever he was now. The constant, unrelenting threat of death was beginning to become more than she could bear.

And she knew Miklos was mad at her, that

he was ready to tear into her for having acted so foolishly. And he would be right. She might have started with good intentions, but they meant nothing. Gunther was dead. A sob escaped her throat.

She fully expected the prince to give her a piece of his mind, was ready to admit how right he was, how foolish she'd been. But the next thing she knew, his arms were warm and strong around her, his presence fortifying as he pulled her to him. His familiar scent comforted her. She let her head rest against his shoulder as she swallowed her tears.

"I shouldn't have left you alone in that room," he said softly.

His warm hand reached under the parka he'd insisted she wear, and smoothed her back. She soaked in his strength. And with each passing moment, she became more and more aware of their bodies touching.

She only had to move her head a fraction of an inch to have her mouth come into contact with his neck. She could feel his pulse as blood rushed under his skin. Her lips tingled, but she didn't move away. She brought a hand up to his chest instead, and sank into the feeling of his arms tightening around her.

Awareness filled out the darkness. The connection between them could not be ignored. It had been there from the very first moment. She had been foolish to deny it.

Heat blossomed inside her and spread through her body.

"Would you mind if I kissed you?" he asked suddenly.

Desire trembled through her. Maybe it was the imminent threat of death, but she wanted him with every ounce of her being, as if his touch was the only anchor left that held her to life. But she didn't want him to see, to know just how badly she needed him.

"Oh, why not. We'll be dead by morning anyway."

"That's the spirit," he said with a chuckle that broke some of the tension between them, but not the sexual tension, which even another avalanche would have had trouble extinguishing at this stage. He put a finger under her chin and tilted her face up to his.

When their lips touched at last, their surroundings fell away.

Warm.

Firm.

Seeking.

He kissed her bottom lip leisurely, like a man who had all the time in the world, when all she wanted was to rush headlong into the denied need between them. The top lip came next, then the corners of her mouth. And when she relaxed at last and sighed in pleasure, his tongue swept inside to touch hers.

Inches of clothes stood between them, but she was more aware of his body than she'd ever been of any other man. Need filled her little by little as he expertly seduced her mouth. That scared her. She didn't want to need him.

She'd come to admit the attraction, then to admit that there was little she could do to ignore it. But giving into some passing attraction and needing a man the way she needed Miklos at this moment were on different planes altogether.

Needing a man gave him power. Needing a man could leave her with a broken heart. Or with a life she'd never wanted, one that would make her miserable.

Startled by the thought, she pulled back a little.

She took a long moment to reassure

herself. No, her heart had nothing to do with this. She wasn't that far gone yet. Her heart was still safe. So when he moved after her and claimed her lips again, she let him.

And maybe she didn't need to think months or years into the future anyway. Maybe all she had—all they had—was this one night. And if that was the case, she wanted to spend it in Miklos's arms.

So she shrugged out of the parka, and after she let it drop to the floor, she was the one who slipped her hands under his sweater and shirt, flattening her greedy palms against the warm skin of his hard abdomen.

He caught his breath.

She smiled into the darkness, then peeled off her sweater.

"I wish I could see you," he said.

"If you could, I probably wouldn't be this brave."

"I've never seen you anything but coura-
geous yet."

Something shifted in her chest. She focused
on the physical side of things between them
instead. She took off her shirt, then the long-
sleeved tee she wore under that.

"You'll catch a cold," he said, but his large
hands ran up her side, caressing her rib cage.

"I'll let you know when I start feeling the
chill."

That must have reassured him, because he
reached to her back to unclasp her bra, then
pulled his hands back to the front and cupped
her breasts. She immediately felt her nipples
harden and pleasure zing through her.

By the time his hot, moist mouth closed
over one nipple, she was so close to the edge
that the sudden, deep draw and the flick of
his tongue nearly sent her over.

He undressed in record time, never fully

losing contact with her. Then he undressed her the rest of the way and pulled her onto his lap so she sat facing him, straddling him, the obvious proof of his desire between them.

"You're a prince. You must have women falling into your bed left and right," she said in a final attempt to gain some perspective, build some defense so she wouldn't fall in love with him right here, right now.

"I'm a prince. Under nearly twenty-four-seven media attention. The potential for astronomical disaster is pretty high with every relationship. Tabloids have fodder for a week if I so much as look at a woman." He cupped her breasts again.

"Are you telling me you're a virgin?" she mocked, pretending that his touch wasn't making her breathless.

She heard a quick, low chuckle.

"Would you go extra gentle with me if I were?" he asked before moving one of his hands to her hip and fitting his lips to her nipple.

She wanted fast and hot and hard. Now.

"Sure." The single word came out on a moan.

"Liar," he said.

Her hands roamed his magnificent body, and soon she, too, wished for some light so that she might see him. He explored her gently but thoroughly, and she felt her body responding to the slightest touch, to each and every kiss. All the delicious tensions grew inside her. When she couldn't take them any longer, she rose up to her knees, and as he guided her with his hands on her buttocks, she fitted herself over him.

There might be no going back after this, she thought and hesitated for a split second, but then his lips captured hers in a soul-wrenching kiss. Maybe there had never been any chance of going back, not from the moment her plane had touched down on the tarmac.

She let her body slide down onto him.

Once he was inside her, he held her in place for a second, his hands on her hips. Not that she could have moved anyway. She needed to catch her breath, needed to adjust to the spreading pleasure of him stretching her.

She thought she would lose it with the first move of his hips, but he seemed to know her body better than she did and somehow cajoled her into staying with him.

It was as though their bodies had been made for each other, they fit perfectly together in every way. She had been a fool to ever think that she'd be able to resist him. This went way beyond resolutions and common sense and her plans for life.

This was life.

Afterward, when she lay spent in his arms, heartbeat against heartbeat, she was stunned by the elemental force that had erupted between them. And still lingered. She had to pull back and catch her breath a little.

But he captured her mouth in one last kiss. Well.

A few more minutes passed before she could move away and put some space between them. She tried to gather her thoughts.

Her brain was clearly not running on enough power yet, because she found herself saying, "When this is over. If we make it. If you still want it. I'll marry you." Then she quickly added. "If it helps the country."

Then she shut up, not quite able to believe that she'd said any of that.

She wasn't sure what she'd expected from

him by way of a response, but it sure as anything wasn't an emphatic "No."

He was dragging his clothes back on.

The chill had definitely returned to the cell.

"What?" She stared at him through the darkness and was frustrated that she could only see his outline but not the expression on his face.

"Under other circumstances," he said with some tension in his voice. "But no."

"What circumstances?" she snapped, grabbing for her own clothes, feeling unexpectedly shaken. She didn't want to be rejected naked.

"It's not what you want."

"Can I be the one to decide what I want?" Then she added, "As you've put it before, I'm willing to make the sacrifice."

"No."

For a second, speech defied her. "You're

too stubborn to be believed. You're completely unreasonable. You know that?"

God save any sane woman from princes.

"I've put your life in danger already." His voice was thick with emotion, but resolution as well.

"Spare me the 'I'm the valiant prince and I will save you from myself' routine."

"Listen, I—"

"Heard enough. No further explanation necessary. I take it back. I don't want to marry you."

She couldn't believe they were fighting when her body was still tingling with pleasure from what they'd done just moments ago. Don't go back there. She tried to focus on the present.

"I do want to marry you," he said distinctly. He was already dressed.

"Would you make up your mind?" She

dragged on her sweater. "I think it's good that we're not getting married. We'd probably strangle each other before the honeymoon was over."

His arm reached for her in the darkness and pulled her hard against his chest. The next second he was kissing her, hard and without any restraint, without end, taking, taking, taking. Only when she had nothing left—no strength in her spine, no air in her lungs—did he let her go.

She was stunned. Dazed. Shocked.

His.

She shook her head to get that crazy thought out.

He swore under his breath and reached for her again, and she steeled herself this time. But she didn't get to find out whether or not she could have resisted. The cell's steel door slammed open. Private time was over.

Chapter Eight

When the three men came in, Miklos's head was still spinning from Judi, his emotions whipped into a maelstrom where she was concerned. But he had to set that aside now, focus on the moment if he were to save them. They would have time together later. He swore to that.

He didn't ask the men why they'd turned against the monarchy. He knew the answer to that: They were following their general, and General Rossi was following someone who'd promised him power. So he asked another question, one that was a million times more important to him. "What is happening with my family?"

"They will remain under guard at Maltmore Castle until tonight," one of them said. He was a captain.

And then they'd be killed. An attack by the very soldiers who were supposed to protect them, probably dressed as rebels. Or maybe an accident of gigantic proportions was planned to take out everyone. Maybe a fire at the castle, or the ceiling of the dining room collapsing as the royal family took supper. The choices were as endless as the general was inventive.

The captain held Miklos's gaze. For a moment, he looked like he was torn over choices he had to make. "Out of all of this, you're the only thing I regret," he said quietly, then squared his shoulders and hardened his face. By the time he walked out the door, he was once again a soldier without emotions.

A crack in the general's plan? Maybe a weakness he could exploit. Miklos looked after the man as the two who'd remained pointed their handguns at Judi and him.

One opened the cell door. He motioned to Judi. "You. Out."

"Put on the coat first," Miklos said and moved toward the door so he could throw himself in the gap if he thought they were trying to separate him from her. No way in hell would he let her go anywhere without him.

She shrugged into the parka and stepped out of the cell. Her hands were tied, and she was gagged again.

Miklos came next, furious that he couldn't do anything. But with a gun pressed against Judi's chest, he didn't even dare look like he was planning a move.

They were shoved up the concrete stairs and to the flatbed military truck that waited for them just outside.

Twilight was settling in.

He scanned as much of the compound as he could see, but couldn't spot the captain. And he didn't have much time to look. Soon they were pushed up into the cab, one armed man on each side of them. Judi was sitting next to the driver, Miklos next to the other man.

He had no idea where the men were taking them and, with the gag, could no longer ask. Still, two against two. If it weren't for the weapons, the odds wouldn't have been bad.

He tried to figure out how much time they had left. They'd taken his watch and cell. But then the driver turned on the ignition, and the radio in the truck came on and it showed the time. Six *p.m.* They had a few hours at best. The captain had talked about this evening.

He looked at the two men, soldiers in the same army he served in, and felt nothing but disgust toward them. They would only look at him when absolutely necessary. They fully knew what they were doing.

But there were other, honorable men among the ones he served with, he was sure of it. He needed to get to those and ask for help. They needed to take back the castle.

He took stock of the cab, every detail. Judi's hands were tied in the front, his in the back. The soldiers thought her the lesser danger, which was also something that could be exploited. There wasn't much else to help them, but he was slowly forming a plan.

When the truck left the general's compound and they were far enough away, rattling down the icy road toward some unknown destination, Miklos cleared his throat. Then he coughed behind the rag in his mouth. Coughed again. Gagged.

He leaned forward and gasped for air. The man to his right bent, gun pressed to Miklos's side, to see what was wrong with him. In a sudden move that he put all his weight behind, Miklos brought his head back, slamming it into the soldier's face, knocking the man out. Since the gun was touching Miklos, he knew exactly where it was without having to turn. With his hands behind his back, he grabbed it, slid his grip to the handle, brought it to his other side and shot at the driver.

Judi was bent as far as she was able— having figured out that he was trying for a break—with her head on her knees. He had no trouble aiming, didn't have to waste a single second with hesitation. The headshot went a little off course, hit the driver's cheek-bone instead of his temple, made a mess.

But Judi had the steering wheel in the next second, her feet on the brake, bringing the truck to a stop before it could have hit a snowcapped boulder.

They stayed motionless for a second, both breathing hard, just looking at each other. He could have looked at her for eternity, but right now time was of the essence.

"Get his knife," he said after a moment. His words sounded unintelligible from behind the gag.

But she understood from the movement of his head. She cut him loose, keeping her gaze on him and away from the men.

He removed her gag first, then his. "Good work." Then he set her hands free.

He opened the door, shoved the man he'd knocked out, jumped to the ground after him, but didn't bother with finishing the job. He had no time and no bullets to spare. He went around the front of the truck and to the driver's side instead, dragged the driver's body out and took the man's seat. He used his sleeve to wipe the blood from the steering wheel.

"Where are we going?" Judi drew as far from the bloody mess as possible, practically pressing herself into the passenger-side door. She was staring at him wide-eyed, clearly shaken, but holding it together.

He stepped on the gas. "There's a military base nearby. We need to pick up a couple of men."

She had blood in her hair and tears in her eyes. Her hands were trembling.

"Hey." He wanted to pull her to him, but was aware that she needed a moment to gather herself. "You did great. Hang in there. It's almost over."

Then he drove like his brother, Lazlo, who not only owned a business that built cars, but in his free time he also raced them.

A half hour passed, mostly in silence, before he reached the base. He hesitated for a second before he pulled up to the gate. What if the general had somehow gained control of all the men?

What if he was walking to his death, taking Judi with him? A million thoughts raced through his head, but that was the one that gave weight to his fears. He did not want to put Judi in any more danger than he already had.

It all came down to what he believed. Could that many people hate his family, hate him? Was the monarchy a leech feeding off the people, a tyrant that kept them down? Were the things the Freedom Council was saying the way the average person felt? Had he been that out of touch with the life of the common people? Had his family?

Even as he asked himself those questions, he knew that, whatever dangers waited for him up ahead, he couldn't back away from them.

There were two guards at the gate.

Both he and Judi were armed, but he wasn't sure Judi could or would use a gun. She still looked stunned from the violence of taking the truck over. But he wouldn't underestimate her. She'd stood her ground at every turn.

He pulled the truck up to the men.

"Major." They saluted him and drew up the gate. "You got away from the kidnappers. Thank God. Can we help?"

They looked wide-eyed at the blood on the window and the blood on his forehead. The cut above his eye had stopped bleeding during the night, but he hadn't dared rubbing the dried clumps off, not wanting to start it bleeding again.

They looked at him with pure joy and relief, not as if they were in cahoots with the general. "Do you require assistance, Major?"

Miklos looked at the open gate, but left the truck idling. "Is General Rossi on base?"

"Yes, Major. He came through five minutes ago."

He hesitated. For the first time ever, he found trusting his people difficult. He slipped his hand off the steering wheel, grabbed the gun on his lap and put his finger on the trigger. "General Rossi has turned traitor. He's the one who had me kidnapped. He's holding the royal family at Maltmore Castle. He's preparing to kill them tonight."

The men couldn't have looked more flabbergasted. "Major?"

He gripped his gun a little tighter as he said, "Time for you to declare your alliance." It struck him how somber his voice sounded.

"Queen and country!" The men shouted as one and snapped their heels together. There hadn't been so much as a split second of hesitation.

Miklos relaxed. "Get in the back."

"Can't leave our post," one of them protested.

"It's an order."

"Yes, Major."

When he reached the middle of the army base, he pulled over by the mess hall. "Go and find men that you trust absolutely. Only the ones that you know for a fact are loyal to the crown. Bring them back here."

The fact that the guards were steadfast gave him hope. There had to be other loyal soldiers. And he had his own men. He hurried across the road, toward his platoon, with Judi close on his heels.

Since darkness had fallen, floodlights lit the base.

"I would try to hide you somewhere until it's all over, but I'm sure our presence on base has already been noted and reported to the general."

"I'd rather stay with you, anyway," she said.

Forever? He wanted to ask, but didn't. He moved on with what he had to do instead. He found his platoon's quarters empty, with a guard posted at the door. "Where are they?" he demanded.

"In the brig. Conduct unbecoming. General's orders."

He could not wait to come face-to-face with the general.

He took off for the small military lockup

on base, was let through without question. The general had probably not expected him to show up here, had not thought of giving instructions to have him seized if he showed up. Or maybe the general had wanted to give just such an order, but couldn't because he didn't have the whole base on his side yet. A thought to give Miklos hope. Still, as he walked into the jail, he wondered if getting out was going to be as easy as getting in.

"I want my platoon released at once," he told the second lieutenant at the desk.

"I'm sorry, Major, I can't. General's orders."

In the army, the general outranked him.

"By order of His Royal Highness, release them." He played his trump card for the first time in more than two decades of his life as a military man.

The lieutenant's eyes went wide. "Yes, Your Highness." He made a call.

The platoon was coming toward him less than two minutes later, anger and outrage etched on every rugged face. These were his closest friends, the ones he'd trained with before he became a captain, and then a major. If anyone stayed loyal, this was the solid core.

"We didn't do a damned thing," Tony said in Italian.

Joe flashed a dirty look at the captain, then looked at Judi with interest. "The general's gone mad."

"It's worse than that." Miklos explained the situation to his men. They swore as they listened, had murder in their eyes before he was done.

While he spoke, they'd quietly surrounded the second lieutenant and his men at the front office. Now Miklos threw a questioning look toward the officer.

"Queen and country!" The man swore his allegiance.

But two of his men gripped their weapons tighter and inched toward the phone. Tony took care of them.

"Lady Judit Marezzi." Miklos introduced her at last. "Lord Marezzi's daughter. Guarding her with your life is going to be your primary objective."

"Yes, Major," the men said as one, a speculative look spreading on some of the faces, knowing grins on others.

"Let's figure out who we can completely trust. Then you and you—" he pointed at Vince and Pete "—are going to find them."

THE BASE LOCKUP WAS A good place to draw back to, since it was fortified to keep people from getting out. But settling in for a siege wasn't Miklos's plan. He had to gather as many faithful men as he could, then head to Maltmore Castle.

He'd sent men to find the general, but he didn't hold much hope that they'd succeed. The general knew the base pretty damn well and had too many supporters here to be easily captured.

His old platoon held thirty men. Four platoons made up the company he'd headed when he'd been a captain. When he became a major, even more soldiers came under his supervision. He was now in charge of a full battalion. If the battalion remained loyal to him, the monarchy would be saved. But he wasn't optimistic enough to count on that.

As more and more men gathered in front of the mess hall across the road, Miklos climbed to the prison's flat roof, cursing the pain that pulsed through his knee. Strange how he'd forgotten all about that injury while he'd been holding Judi in his arms back in their cell.

Slipping into that memory was tempting. He glanced back. She sat on the roof, in cover, out of the range of any rifles on the ground. Her gaze held absolute trust. He drank that in for as long as he could before turning to the waiting men.

"You know me," he started in a voice loud enough to reach them. "You know what I stand for. Some of you have served with me for two decades. We did the drills to fight any enemy that could threaten the country we love."

"Yeah."

"Damn right we did."

He heard individual voices of agreement from the group.

"Today's the day we have to fight that fight. And it's worse than we ever expected. Your queen and my brothers have already been captured. They might have already been killed." His voice dropped on the last word. "And the enemy came from within."

An outraged growl rippled through the men.

"Who's the traitor?" a number of men shouted.

He knew the guards and his men must have passed that news on already, but he also knew that the soldiers needed confirmation. They were loyal to the army, to their superior officers. They needed to hear a distinct charge from him.

"General Rossi."

A roar rose, mingling with the sound of new people approaching. The general's men were bearing down on them and had opened fired without warning.

"Queen and country!" the soldiers in front of the mess hall shouted as the fight for the base, and for Valtria, began.

SHE HAD COME TO VALTRIA for a fun vacation and found herself in the middle of a war. Hours after she'd made love with a prince.

Life could not get stranger, Judi thought as she sat in the cab of yet another military truck with Miklos. He'd left the taking back of the base to those who'd remained on his side, taking as many as he could, the ones whose loyalty he could personally vouch for—a hundred soldiers—to save his family.

The general had escaped ahead of them.

The wind hadn't blown the snow clouds this far east yet, so the sky was clear, the full moon reflecting off the sparkling white snow that covered everything.

They were crossing a valley, and as she took in the hillside, she spotted a beautiful building with turrets and towers. It all looked so peaceful that hope leaped into her heart.

Maybe there would not be a fight after all. Maybe the general had figured out that he could not stand against Miklos. Maybe he and his traitorous troops had cleared out already and everything was well.

God knew, Miklos was in no shape to lead any liberating forces. He was badly banged up, and she couldn't remember the last time he might have slept.

"Is that Maltmore?"

Miklos flashed her a funny look, considered her for a long moment as the truck rattled over the frozen ground. He took a minute between giving orders over the radio. He'd been organizing the upcoming fight since they'd left the base. "That's your castle."

She stared at him. Okay, obviously, life could get stranger, in fact.

"I don't have a castle."

"It's the Marezzi ancestral seat."

That took a second to digest. "Why don't I know about this?"

"You'll inherit it upon marriage."

"If this is a trick," she said before she remembered that he'd already told her that he didn't want to marry her, so he couldn't be using this as a bribe or something. Man, but it was hard to think straight under the circumstances.

"Or on your twenty-ninth birthday," he added. "It's been held in a trust since your father's death."

"I turn twenty-nine next week." The very thing that had brought her here. She'd wanted to discover her roots. From where she was sitting right now, roots were way overrated. The trip had been a nightmare.

Except for Miklos.

"Then your father's Valtrian barristers," he

was saying in all seriousness, "will be contacting you with the details next week. You can count on that."

Okay, then. Sheesh. Why didn't she think of that? Maybe because inheriting and owning castles fell a tad outside of her life experience. Just a tad.

"Who lives there now?" she asked, marveling that her brain even worked.

"An Austrian nobleman. He's been a very good tenant."

"You kept track of that?" How sweet.

"The chancellor usually included a brief note in his annual reports about you." His face darkened.

And so did her heart at the mention of the strange old man. But she still couldn't take her eyes from the hillside. Her castle. Seriously. Like nobody in the past twenty-nine years of her life thought she needed to know about this? Aunt Viola had a lot to answer for.

She looked over the white limestone of the walls that seemed to glow in the moonlight. Her. Castle. The place looked like something straight out of a fairy tale.

"How old is it?"

"Five hundred plus. Older than the country you've been living in." He flashed her an amused look.

And she could have cried that she was only now realizing that she had this kind of heritage. Not the money, but the whole country, the people. She often felt alone and lonely in D.C., having no relatives beyond Aunt Viola anywhere near. And now she found out that she had all this ancestry here. It wasn't the same as having living grandparents and cousins, but it was something.

Then the valley widened and they came

upon a castle ten times as large and majestic in the distance.

"Maltmore Castle," he said.

About to come under siege, she realized as she took in the tanks and military vehicles that surrounded it. She flinched as the first weapons were fired.

"I want you to stay here and stay hidden," Miklos said as he had the driver pull out of the convoy and stop the truck. "I'll leave the men with you."

He got out, and she went after him. Half a dozen members of his platoon were in the truck's bed. The rest rode in the other vehicles.

"No." Not that she was heroic. But truth be told, she felt safest with him. He hadn't let her down yet.

"I'm sorry, princess." He drew her into his arms and kissed her thoroughly.

In front of his men.

Some of whom made embarrassing noises.

He glared at them when he pulled back. "That's not up for negotiation," he told her. And then he was moving away from her and getting into the back of another truck.

Oh, hell no. He was so not going to leave her behind. She lurched after him, but was caught in quick order. "I'm going with him. Let me go!"

His buddies, every bit as obstinate as the prince himself, wouldn't release her.

"Do not leave me here!" she shouted after him.

He didn't even look back.

Fury came first. Then she felt defeated for all of about five minutes. Then looked over her guard. They looked as unhappy as she felt.

For a second, she considered whether to go with nice or nasty. She didn't feel nice at the moment.

"Boy, you guys must be bad." She sneered at them. "I guess when it comes to a fight, he really doesn't want you to be watching his back."

The men glowered at her. They were big and brawny and more than a little intimidating. She ignored all of that.

"Would this be like a demotion?" she pushed.

Their lips thinned.

"I'm not royal," she pointed out. "I don't even feel all that Valtrian. I'm American."

The look in their eyes told her what they thought of that. Probably that her father was rolling in his grave. She bit back a sigh. It couldn't be helped.

"What happened to all that Queen and country stuff? Shouldn't rushing to the Queen's aid be your first priority?"

If their jaws were any tighter, their teeth

would start breaking, she reflected. Murder glinted clearly in a number of eyes. They all wore camouflage gear and were armed to the teeth.

"You're not going into the fight," the one Miklos had called Vince said.

"We could go together. You could keep an eye on me and help the Queen."

"Not going to happen."

She sulked for a full minute. "I could get away from you, you know."

"No, you couldn't." Vince didn't look amused.

She took in the six of them. He was right. She couldn't. "We could pretend I did."

They went back to glowering.

"I got away from your precious prince." She wagged her head. Okay, from the inn. And Miklos hadn't been there at the time, but still, it counted.

She saw at least two sets of lips twitch, and one blond eyebrow shot up before it was brought under control.

"The point is, since I got away from him, he would believe that I could get away from you. So you wouldn't get into trouble."

It was a testament to how miserable the men felt at having been left out of the fight that they looked like they were considering her plan.

"If the Queen and the princes are killed, it's not going to matter whether or not I stay alive," she said quietly, a dull pain spreading in her chest at the prospect.

If anything happened to Miklos…

He'd left her behind. Oh, he was insufferable. What did she care? Except that she did, and it went beyond not wanting to see anyone get hurt.

Miklos, for all his faults, had reached a

spot inside her heart that nobody had ever been able to touch before.

She caught that thought and tried to breathe.

Oh God. She was going mad. She'd only known him for days. It wasn't possible to fall for someone in such a short amount of time.

Except that she'd felt the connection between them from the first moment.

The sound of gunfire filled the air at the castle.

A battle. She was standing on the edge of the battlefield and desperate to go in there. What was wrong with her? She had lost all reasonable thought. There could be no doubt about that.

She didn't care.

"Please?" she asked with all the desperation in her heart. "I distinctly remember that Valtria has a history of warrior princesses."

Their story was one her father had told her

when she was little, her favorite, not one she would ever forget. And it occurred to her all of a sudden that they could very well have been the inspiration for her princess video games without her ever having made a conscious connection.

"Remember the warrior princesses?" she demanded.

The men simply glared at her again. They were nothing if not consistent. They were clearly not impressed with her knowledge of the past. In fact, Vince looked annoyed enough to wring her neck himself.

"What will he do to you if you disobey?" she taunted.

"Court martial if he doesn't like you as much as I think he does," Joe told her. "If he's in love?" He shrugged. "He'll kill us dead."

"He doesn't love me," she protested. The

idea was completely ridiculous. "He doesn't even want to marry me. He told me that."

They didn't look convinced.

"You have two choices," she explained with a patience she didn't feel. "You don't go after him to help, and he gets killed. Or you go after him and save him, but he'll be mad at you and he might come after you. What's more important, your life or the prince's? I'm not afraid for my life. Are you that afraid for yours?"

And it looked like she had finally reached them, at last, and she hadn't underestimated their devotion to Miklos.

After a moment of silent communication between the men, Joe and Vince moved toward the cab.

"Get in the back," Vince snapped.

HE KNEW GENERAL ROSSI had to be some-where at the castle, and Miklos was impatient to catch up with the traitor, but he hadn't seen the man yet. The general had sent his troops to fight Miklos and his soldiers back at the base, and used the chaos to leave. But, at least while his men were kept busy back there by those who were still faithful to the crown, they couldn't be coming here, providing backup for the general.

At least Judi was safe, away from all the fighting. Ignoring the pain in his knee, Miklos lunged forward from the cover of his truck and took aim, shot, hit his target. They were making progress. In a few minutes, they would reach the gate.

They had enemies inside, too. The sounds of fighting in the castle yard were unmistakable. That was the enemy he was worried about. The ones closest to his family. They fought with the loyal servants and guards on the inside, while the soldiers who'd gone over to the general's side were holding off Miklos's rescue forces.

He aimed and picked off another man.

The last time the castle had seen any fighting was in World War II. A couple of employees had fathers who'd fought to defend this very gate and these very walls, first against the Germans, then the Russians. He couldn't stand the thought that the castle could fall to an internal enemy after all it had survived over the centuries. He couldn't stand the thought of his family in mortal danger in there, while he was out here, making painfully slow progress.

A bullet pinged off the hood of the truck, and he ducked. He limped around the vehicle and saw the sniper on a parapet. His handgun wasn't up to a job like that, so he swung his rifle off his shoulder.

He'd just finished off the sniper when he turned, his instincts alerting him that someone was coming up behind him.

Judi.

He swore under his breath and glared at his men, who were holding a protective formation around her. "I'm going to shoot you myself," he told them and had the pleasure of watching those battle-hardened men pale.

Vince shot him a pleading look. "There was no holding her back."

He shook his head, not that he doubted the truth of the statement. He turned the glare on Judi.

She pulled herself straight. "I've got two words for you. Warrior princess."

And damn if she didn't look it at the moment. Her eyes flashed with determination, her hair pulled back, her fingers closed around the gun he'd left with her.

"You don't know how to shoot," he reminded her, feeling trapped by the moment. She should never have come here.

"You taught me. The safety's off. All I have to do is pull the trigger." She lifted the gun and motioned as she talked.

His men ducked.

He caught her arm and pushed it down. "When the safety's off, the gun is always pointing to the ground, except when you're shooting."

A second of embarrassment flashed across her face, but then she stuck her chin out. "I knew that."

Defiant to the last, he thought. And then he thought, *I could fall in love with this woman.*

But as the fighting intensified around them, he didn't have much time to ponder that. And he sure wasn't going to make any comments on any possible future relationship between the two of them while she had a loaded gun in her hands.

"Keep down, and keep out of trouble," he told her.

"We're in the middle of a siege," she pointed out.

He glared at her. "I know that."

Then a shout drew his attention, and he realized that the gate had been breached. The truck behind which he'd hidden to shoot moved forward. He, Judi and his men followed in its cover.

"When we reach the inside, there's a little stone guardhouse tucked into the base of the South Tower. I'm personally locking you in there."

Which was a good plan, but it didn't happen that way. He was hit the second he stepped through the gate. The bullet went through his right hand. The gun he held disappeared. But he could see plenty of blood and shards of bone, and in that instant he knew that was the end of the hand and his military career.

His men shoved him into the guardhouse, too hard. Being hit had already thrown him off balance. As he lurched forward, his head cracked against the wall. His ears were ringing as he slid to the ground.

BULLETS WERE STILL flying in every direction. Judi knew only that Miklos had been hurt. She threw herself over him in a very Jacqueline Kennedy sort of moment. Then his men were there, bending over them, and she registered at last the blood covering his hand.

Vince immediately ripped off the sleeve of his own uniform to staunch the bleeding. "Hold tight. Here."

She did.

He radioed for a military ambulance, which under the current circumstances might or might not be able to get to them.

Miklos groaned.

"He needs space to breathe," she said when she realized there were eight of them crammed into a guardhouse meant for two.

The men stepped outside and took up positions.

Vince called back, "Help's on the way. Keep him comfortable."

How did you keep comfortable a man who was bleeding to death? Her heart raced as panic squeezed her chest. He couldn't die. He was a good man. He didn't deserve this. This was all so incredibly unfair. Her eyes burned with unshed tears.

"I'm sorry. I'm so sorry." A sob escaped her throat as she cradled his head in her lap. "Everyone I love dies. I should never have…

Everyone I love dies," she repeated. It was true. It was all her fault. By loving him, she had cursed him. "I'm sorry. I'm sorry. I'm sorry."

"Sorry enough to obey me next time?" he asked in a rough tone, as if waking from a dream.

She blinked away enough tears so she could see him.

His eyes were open.

"Fat chance of that." She sniffed.

He smiled. "That's my princess."

"I'm not your princess." How could he make her think that he was dying when all he was doing was coming up with more ways to aggravate her?

"But you will be."

"I'll think about it."

"You love me." His sexy smile put in an appearance.

"Did I say that?"

"You bet."

"I was under duress." She was an emotional basket case. And considering all that had happened to her since her plane had landed, who could blame her?

He was laughing. She couldn't see how. His right hand was about blown off. She knew what that would mean to a man as physical as he was.

Vince popped his head in, pulled a white pill from a small pocket on his belt. "Good, you're conscious enough to take this. You better swallow it, Major. I would have given it to you sooner, but you fainted."

If looks could kill, Vince would have been a smoking heap of ashes on the threshold.

"I did not faint." Miklos enunciated each word with care.

"Of course not, Major." But Vince's eyes were dancing.

"You hoodlums knocked my head against the stone."

"Sorry, Major."

"I don't need the damn pill."

"The adrenaline will wear off in about a minute."

Or sooner, Judi thought as Miklos's face suddenly turned ashen.

They were so not going to argue about whether or not he was taking the damn pill. She called forth her inner warrior princess she'd been referring to so often in the past hour and snatched the pill from Vince's hand. "Open up, or I swear to everything that's holy, I'll…"

He gave her a grim look but did as she asked.

"She's scary," Vince said, then caught himself. "Sorry, Major."

"No offense taken. I like that about her." Miklos sat up at last, gritting his teeth, making sure he didn't lean on his bad hand. "What's going on out there?"

"Slaughter," Vince said with disgust. "But the whole platoon is here at the guardhouse. We're going to keep this position secure."

"Damn right. And if you let her go again, you'll answer to me with your life. All of you," Miklos said and stood with a lurch, grabbing Vince's rifle with his left hand.

"No." Judi reached for him, stunned at this latest move.

But he already had his back to her, talking to Vince. "Have you seen my brothers?"

"I might have heard Lazlo's voice from the North Tower."

Miklos nodded and moved forward, sparing only a brief but potent look in Judi's direction. "You stay here."

"Permission to come with you, Major?" Vince was right by his side.

Miklos stepped out into the desperate fight in the courtyard without bothering to answer.

Chapter Nine

He'd been gone for an hour. A lot could happen in an hour. Judi tried not to think of any specifics. He was practically maimed already, for heaven's sake. Why Miklos felt the need to go back to fighting was beyond her. Him and his damned sense of duty.

She went to the door and opened it a crack to see if she might not be able to catch a glimpse of the prince, only to have it slammed back in her face. Which meant that his men were still out there, guarding her. Good to know. Because the battle didn't sound like it was winding down anytime soon.

"Get down!" someone bellowed from outside.

But before she could do anything, an explosion shook the guardhouse, knocking her from her feet. The boom came from somewhere above them, probably someone tossing a hand grenade on the upper floors. She huddled in the corner as the walls shook, some bricks falling from the ceiling. Dust and masonry bits drizzled around her, making her cough. Instinct pushed her to bolt for the door before the ceiling collapsed altogether, but the sounds of battle outside held her in place.

Trapped.

Where was her safe, familiar little cubicle crammed full of graphic-design gadgets? What was she doing in a castle under siege? She'd made up these kinds of things for her video games. They weren't supposed to happen for real.

"We need another place to wait this out." Vince burst in to check on her, and noted the unstable rocks above. His gaze settled on the small, wooden door at Judi's back. "Stand behind me."

And when Judi moved out of the way, he shot the lock off the door. He looked into the area behind it, then up. "The South Tower."

"Do you think it's safer up there than down here?" Didn't the boom of that grenade come from up there? She would have preferred to stay where Miklos had left her. She didn't want him to have trouble finding her when he came back. Please, God, let him come back. Let him come back without any new injuries.

"I don't hear any sounds of fighting from above." Vince shouted out instructions to the other men.

Four moved into the staircase, led by Joe. Then Vince motioned for Judi. The rest of them came up behind her, defending her from behind. She felt like the president, surrounded by Secret Service officers—an experience she could have lived without. Another reminder of what her life would be like if their arranged marriage took place.

Which seemed the least of her problems at the moment.

"You should go and protect the prince," she told the men.

"Don't start on that again." Vince flashed her a discouraging look. "The major can take care of himself. We'll do exactly as he instructed."

They were all tough guys, every last one of them. They would not have followed a weak leader. If Miklos were anything else but the kind of man he was, he could not have inspired this kind of loyalty. He really was a man like no other: strong, honorable…

She didn't have time to ponder Miklos's fearless nature. Vince was nudging her forward. The spiral staircase was ancient and so narrow that it only allowed one person at a time. Would have been good to know whether the explosion caused any structural damage.

"Keep your head down," Vince instructed, not looking particularly concerned about the condition of the stairs.

They stole ahead step by step, the staircase seeming to go on forever. At least they didn't meet any enemy. She was starting to get dizzy from going around and around by the time they finally reached the top.

She was instructed to sit behind the stone parapet and stay still, while the men engaged and picked off some of the enemy from their higher positions. She hugged her knees and prayed for Miklos and his family, frustrated that she could do nothing to help them, that she knew nothing about where he was, what was happening to him.

Then she spotted holes in the parapet at regular intervals, and she moved up to one to look out. She could see some of the open area outside the castle. Nobody was out there save the fallen and a couple of abandoned military vehicles and two burned-out tanks. The fight had moved inside the castle walls in the last hour or so.

Floodlights lit up the castle, and men fought as if by daylight.

She slid to another peephole and could see a section of roof. She was looking for a view of the castle yard, so she was about to move on when she noticed movement on the edge of the roof. The next moment Miklos appeared, balancing perilously on the old, ceramic roof tiles. He held the rifle in his left hand, standing straight and tall, his wide shoulders outlined against the sky. The bandage on his right hand was soaked through with blood.

"Miklos!" Her voice was swallowed by the din around them.

She watched as he found sure purchase for his feet and turned his back to her, determination in every move. He looked ready to face anything, but she knew that he had to be exhausted, had to be weakening from blood loss, slowed by pain, dulled by whatever drug Vince had given him.

In a word, he had to be a mess. A total and complete mess. But he had to be out there. He was too damn stubborn to do anything less. If it weren't so futile, she would have screamed at him.

He needed to leave the battle to the rest of the men and find shelter somewhere. He needed to stay still and hold that hand up to slow the bleeding. And then it occurred to her that maybe that was why he had sought the roof. Maybe just this once, he'd decided to be reasonable.

She watched him. *Sit down. Rest.*

But he stood there, focused on something she couldn't see. Tension knotted her muscles. He looked like he was waiting for something. Whatever trouble it was, he was in no shape to face it.

She gasped when, in the next second, a dozen enemy soldiers vaulted up to the roof to fight him.

MIKLOS WAS BADLY outnumbered, and his aim was terrible with his left hand. His father had made sure that all of his sons could fence with both hands, the sport a royal tradition, but nobody had ever thought to teach the princes to shoot left-handed. Something he would have to start practicing, he acknowledged with dismay, as pain throbbed through his right hand.

He was using the gun as a deterrent more than anything else. He squeezed off a couple of rounds and hit one man purely by accident. The rest were closing in on him. Ducking bullets, he kept moving. Damn, but he didn't want to die on this roof. He needed to find the general, capture him and have him call his men off. It was the only way to stop the bloodshed.

His people were dying all over the castle. He had no idea where his family was.

He retreated, shooting wildly, forcing his enemies to scatter on the roof. When gunfire came from the South Tower, he ducked again, thinking someone was trying to get him from behind. But instead, three enemy soldiers fell.

He glanced up and saw Vince and the guys. What were they doing up there? He didn't see Judi. His chest tightened as he tried to get a better look.

A bullet whizzed by his ear, reminding him that he couldn't afford to be distracted. He shot back and, while his men from the roof covered him, ran to the opposite side of the roof and slid to the balcony below, sending some tiles crashing to the courtyard.

He paid little attention to them. He thought of what was ahead of him. He and his brothers had played in every corner of the castle in their childhood. He knew its every nook by heart.

Sounds of fighting came from the servants' quarters. For a moment he hesitated. Instinct pushed him to go and check on Judi, but logic told him that the best way to save her was to find the general and end the battle. He ran toward the sound of guns.

The hallways were narrower here, the floor tile instead of marble, the light fixtures cast iron instead of the Swarovski crystal chandeliers that graced the lower floors. The doors were plain oak, only six feet tall instead of twelve, no decorative raised panels on them, no hand-painted scenes from the country's historical past.

Which was why the young princes used to love to play up here back in the day, away from the strict formality of the main floors of the castle. And the servants spoiled them rotten with sweets and other treats on the frequent occasions when they'd been able to escape their eagle-eyed governesses.

Some of those servants were even now fighting in the courtyard. Some had already been killed.

He ran, making as little noise as possible.

The ruckus of gunfire helped muffle the sound his boots made on the hundred-year-old tile.

He found his brothers in the hall outside the servants' bedrooms that took up the back hallway of the top floor. They were locked in a gunfight with a dozen or so men at the top of the staircase at the end of the hall. The princes cheered when he came around the corner.

"Sorry I'm late." He shot at the enemy blindly while checking over his brothers. Blood all over the place, but nobody looked badly injured. "Mother?" He ducked behind the marble table they were using for cover.

"In her quarters," Janos responded then popped up to let a round fly. A shout on the other end confirmed that he'd hit his target. He always did, whether it was target shooting or golf. The sports papers didn't call him the Devil of the Big Green for nothing.

"Where is the castle guard?" Miklos asked. He'd barely seen any of them around. Fifty of them were in service at any given moment when the royal family was at Maltmore.

"With her. Guarding her." Lazlo was leaning heavily on his right leg. He fearlessly raced the cars his company built and had crushed his left knee two years before in a fiery crash. "What happened to your hand?"

"Bullet." Miklos shrugged, then glared at Arpad. "Why aren't you with her?"

He was the crown prince, damn it, didn't he understand? He would be taking over the country soon. He could not risk his life in a fight like this.

Arpad, never one to be intimidated, glared back. "Where in hell have you been? We thought you'd already been killed."

And the look on his brothers' faces told

Miklos that they'd been just as worried about him as he'd been about them.

No time to explain. "General Rossi betrayed us," he said between two shots, then ducked as bullets whizzed overhead. He glanced back, making sure nobody had followed him from the roof, but didn't see a soul. His men must have picked off that batch from the tower.

But did they still have Judi? Was she safe? He gripped his weapon tighter.

"General Rossi? Are you sure?" Benedek, too well-meaning and, being an architect and a dreamer, not exposed as much to the darker side of life as some of the other princes, asked.

"He's here," was all Miklos said.

Lazlo looked grim. "We have to let the palace guard know not to let him near Mother."

"I'll go." Miklos immediately volunteered.

But Arpad decided to pull rank. "We're the Brotherhood, remember? We'll go together."

Which made sense, gave them a better chance of succeeding, but Miklos didn't have to like it.

They popped up to shoot together, then ducked back down.

Benedek swore. "I'm out of bullets."

Miklos stared. Benedek never swore. He was the mildest man among them.

"Me, too," said Janos.

Miklos checked his own magazine. A half-dozen rounds left.

They had no way to get more bullets or other weapons. Nothing but the servants' rooms up here and... A sudden idea gave him hope. "Does Monsieur Maneaux still live in the castle?"

Their old fencing master had come from France, but became a Valtrian through and through, to the point that instead of retiring back to Provence, where he'd been born, he'd stayed on to restore old weapons.

"Last door on the right," Benedek said. "We're reconstructing the fresco of the Battle of Karman at the Royal Opera House. I talked to him not long ago about the weapons in the scene." He had a formidable eye for detail and the determination to see all his creations done to perfection.

Miklos looked to the last door on the right, which was the farthest from them. To reach it, they had to come out from behind cover.

"Let's go," Arpad ordered.

"I'll go first," Miklos said. "You stay in the middle."

They stared each other down until Lazlo, a daredevil to the end, darted forward with his characteristic limp, and the rest of the brothers were forced to focus on covering him. They came up with guns blazing and charged as one, the Brotherhood of the Crown, and pushed the enemy back.

They had a moment of reprieve when they reached their old fencing master's room, but their situation now was even more dire than before. The charge had used up most of the ammunition they had left.

Miklos tossed his empty rifle and reached for one of the historic swords on the wall instead. Early twentieth century. He checked the blade, found it sharp, then looked for the point of balance and realized that the weapon would be perfect for his left hand. His brothers were testing swords as well.

Grinning, the lot of them.

Miklos rolled his eyes when they started to form a circle, but when they cried, "Duty and honor, our lives for the people and the crown!" Miklos shouted the oath of the Brotherhood with them.

They used what few bullets they had to take out the enemy waiting for them in the hallway. Miklos finished off the last guy with his sword, using a weapon like that for real instead of practice for the first time. His respect for his ancestors immediately increased. Pushing cold steel into a man when he was at arm's reach, holding his gaze as he went down, was vastly different than shooting a gun from a hundred feet away.

He pulled away. Arpad shouted. Then the brothers were running down the servants' staircase toward the queen's quarters.

He caught sight of the guardhouse through one of the windows, saw the intense fighting in front of it, spotted four of his men dead on the ground. The enemy probably thought that his men were defending him, that he was in there. It would be only a matter of time before they broke through and found Judi. If she were still alive.

A ball of ice formed in his chest at the thought.

The brothers ran forward, met a small group of enemy soldiers who were using their rifles as clubs. They, too, were out of bullets. The six princes with their skill at sword fighting made quick work of them.

Then they were outside the back door of the queen's quarters. Two dozen royal guards blocked the entry, but they immediately let the princes through. Arpad warned them of General Rossi's betrayal.

"Have you seen him?" Miklos asked as he passed through.

"No, Your Highness," one of the guards responded.

Good. They were in time then.

Inside the spacious parlor they entered were six more guards, along with the captain of the guards. He immediately gave his report.

"I'm in radio contact. The tide is turning. We have the upper hand almost everywhere except at the base of the South Tower. The army base has been taken back. More loyal troops are on their way."

"The queen is well?" Benedek asked.

"She's with her ladies in waiting, sequestered in her bedroom."

Miklos inspected his brothers. Janos had the least amount of blood on him; the small stains on his sleeve were barely noticeable. "You check on her." No way was he going in there with his hand dripping blood.

Janos took off, looking eager to go. And Miklos suspected it wasn't all about their mother. Rumor had it he had his eye on one of the queen's ladies. He was probably as worried about her as Miklos was about Judi.

Pain pulsed up his arm. The drug Vince had given him was clouding his mind. He regretted taking it, would rather feel the sharp edge of pain and be in full command of his faculties if they were to win this battle.

"We'll need weapons," Arpad was telling the captain.

The guards immediately shared their arsenal with the princes.

The dozen men, the guards and the princes, were reflected in the gilded mirrors that covered the parlor's walls, giving the impression of a much larger force Miklos wished were real.

Janos came back, reporting that the queen was well, given the circumstances. She was aware of what was going on to some extent, but was being shielded from the severity of the fight. "Dr. Arynak is with her."

"You stay with her, too. She might need you," Miklos told his brothers. "I'm going to the South Tower."

"Collecting your princess?" Lazlo wiggled his eyebrows. "How charmingly old-fash-ioned. Prince Charming riding to the rescue."

His brothers were all grinning and flashing him looks full of meaning. Secretly, they were all probably happy that he was the first to lose his freedom and not one of them, instead. He had thought of it in those terms when he'd first been given news of Judi's imminent arrival to the country, but his opinion had changed drastically since.

Istvan, the cultural anthropologist, was mumbling something about mating rituals in different cultures. In response, Arpad made some lip-smacking noises.

Juveniles, every last one of them. God help the monarchy. But when Miklos moved toward the door, they were right behind him.

"You stay," he said. "Especially you." He glared at Arpad.

"Just walking you to the door." His older brother humored him.

But they all walked out with him.

Janos flashed a reassuring grin. "We'll just walk you to the end of the hallway."

Which was a blatant lie. They had no intention of letting him go alone. Miklos was sure of that, but didn't have time to argue with them.

The rest of the royal guard stood in front of the main entrance of the queen's quarters. Some wanted to go with the princes, but Arpad categorically refused. They were to stay and protect the queen and the ladies of the court.

The princes got as far as the top of the stairs before they were first fired upon. His heart nearly stopped when Arpad went down.

Miklos shot back, holding the attackers at bay. "Take him back," he yelled at Janos. "He's the damn crown prince." Dammit. This was not supposed to happen. Shoulder-shot, he registered. "Make a compress!"

Janos and Istvan took Arpad back. He looked more frustrated than in pain, even though blood was running down his arm in rivulets.

"I'm good," he said. "I can still go."

But his siblings weren't impressed. All Arpad could do was shoot Miklos a dirty look as the other two forcibly dragged him off.

Miklos forged forward, Lazlo and Benedek behind him. A businessman race-car driver and an architect. The two youngest of the brothers, the twins. If anything happened to them on his watch, his mother was never going to forgive him.

He used the rifle he had received from the royal guard, then his sword when he was close enough to the enemy. He had always been the best swordsman among the brothers.

They fought their way down to the ground level, only meeting small pockets of resistance. Bodies littered the stairs. The courtyard was where the fighting was at its fiercest. They threw themselves into the melee, loyal soldiers immediately grouping around them.

He glanced up to the South Tower. He still couldn't see Judi, nor could he see any of his men up there anymore. He needed to figure out what had happened to them.

He uttered a fierce cry and charged into the battle.

MIKLOS'S MEN HEADED down the stairs the second they saw him come from the main building. Judi was kept protected at the back.

He was still alive. He was still alive. She kept repeating that to herself. She just about had a heart attack when he'd disappeared on the other side of the roof earlier. She'd thought that he had fallen, so she'd spent the last hour imagining him lying broken on cobblestones somewhere below.

But he was in the castle yard, fighting. *Still alive.*

There were only nine of his platoon left. She could barely stand that thought, knowing all the rest had died for her. The loss was inconceivable. They had gone one by one into the staircase to hold the enemy back from reaching the top of the tower.

They were pushing that enemy back now. They met with Miklos in the nearly collapsed guardhouse. He had a fierce-looking sword in his left hand, like a hero of old, and was using that to fight. When he saw her, he seemed to gain new strength. He cut down the few enemies that still stood between them.

Then they were moving outside, back toward the savage fighting in the yard. The men formed a circle around her. The battle was in its final stages, everyone bloody and exhausted.

"Give me a gun. I demand a gun!" she yelled.

The men ignored her.

"Take the rifle." Mikos offered the weapon slung across his right shoulder. She had to slip it off, as he had a sword in one hand, and the other one wasn't working just now. It was ready to go; all she had to do was squeeze the trigger. Which she did, aiming at a soldier who was shooting at their small group from the top of the castle gate. She shot until she saw him tumble.

Endless minutes elapsed before their group passed through the bloodshed and reached the main building. Loyal troops who were pushing the enemy back from the ground floor immediately formed a shield around them.

"The castle is three-quarters ours again, Your Highnesses," one of them said, and Judi realized that at least some of the men with Miklos were his brothers.

When she looked closer, she realized that two looked exactly alike. The royal twins, she thought, recognizing them at last. They were both incredibly handsome. The tabloids hadn't done them justice.

That anyone would risk his life for her boggled her mind to start with, but that royal princes would be running to her rescue… It seemed beyond the realm of possibility.

"My brothers Lazlo," Miklos introduced the one who had a slight limp, "and Benedek."

The architect, she thought, and was immediately charmed when they apologized that they were too bloody to kiss her hand. Gentlemen in the middle of bloody murder. They sure were princes.

The whole group was marching up the stairs. She tried not to squirm and be too embarrassed as the twins openly checked her out and silently communicated with each other.

Then Miklos stopped in front of a gilded door. "These are my quarters," he told her. "You go and check on Arpad," he said to his brothers.

Half the soldiers who'd followed them in stayed with Miklos, the other half went with the other princes.

Then the richly painted, twelve-foot-high doors in front of her swung open and the opulence of the place left her speechless. They were in a large receiving room filled with the most beautiful furniture, the twenty-foot-high ceiling soaring above, a ten-foot fireplace on the wall opposite them. The walls were hung with tapestries that depicted hunting scenes. The whole room was done in silver and brown with royal blue used as the accent color.

Everything was incredibly masculine and breathtakingly elegant.

The quiet beauty of the room was a complete contrast to the raging battle in the courtyard, to the grime on both herself and Miklos, to the bloody bandage on his hand. Since she'd entered, she had a feeling that she didn't belong here. But right at this moment, Miklos looked like he didn't quite belong, either.

It made her feel better.

She had little time to admire her surroundings, however, or to relax. The next second she was in Miklos's arms, and he was kissing her.

His passion was hot and fierce. It possessed her. She had never been as happy or willing to give herself. All her fear, all the stress of the last couple of days, disappeared and released a huge wave of energy that turned into sexual energy between them.

She wanted him with the same fervor that he wanted her. Right now, right here. On the floor, even; she didn't care.

But he picked her up, and long moments passed before she remembered his injured arm and began to protest. By that time they were in his bedroom and he was laying her on his enormous royal bed.

His mouth possessed hers. She gave herself to him. Would it be so terrible to be married to me? he'd asked not long ago. Not if it would be like this. She wanted him. She couldn't remember wanting any other man so much.

She ran her hands up his strong arms, over his back, impatient for more. She wanted to feel his full weight on her as he covered her.

But he didn't join her on the bed.

"Rest," he told her when he pulled away, breathing as hard as she was.

Fevered tension stretched between them. Rest was the last thing on either of their minds. She could still feel his lips crushing down on hers, and she wanted more. She wanted him to hold her, wanted to hold him until the reality that they were both alive had a chance to sink in.

"It's not safe to let our guard down. Not yet," he said with frustration clear in his voice. With effort, he pulled back from the bed.

She tried to get her racing heart under control.

"There's a bathroom through there." He pointed to another door. "You can clean up if you want."

"Your hand?"

"It'll be fine for a little longer yet."

"No, it won't! Miklos, please listen to me. This is senseless."

"My people need me."

"They'll need you even more after this is all over. Let the soldiers finish."

"I'm a soldier," he reminded her.

"You're an injured man. You're a prince. You have a duty to stay alive, dammit."

A pained smile played at the corner of his lips. "Chancellor Hansen would have said the same thing." His face clouded at the mention of the name.

He went back for his rifle, which she'd

dropped when they'd come in, and brought it to her. "Lock the door behind me and don't let anyone in unless you hear my voice. The guards will stay outside. If anyone comes through that door, don't ask questions, just shoot them."

"You can't be going back to the battle." Desperation pushed her off the bed at last.

He bent to kiss her again, briefly this time, as if not trusting himself.

"Don't go. Didn't that guy say that they had three-quarters of the castle back? Please don't leave me. I couldn't stand if anything happened to you," she admitted.

His gaze swirled with dark heat. But he turned from her anyway.

"What happened to your family?" she asked as it suddenly occurred to her that she'd only seen two of his brothers.

He hesitated, then turned back. Warmth

filled his eyes. "My mother is well-pro-tected. My brothers are a rough lot. They can take care of themselves."

And so could he. She knew that, but it didn't make watching him go any easier. "Be careful. Stay safe. Come back to me."

"I plan on it."

On his way out, he walked to the bathroom to check it. And from the way he suddenly froze, she immediately knew that something was terribly wrong.

Chapter Ten

Judi took a step back, gripping the gun hard, fighting the urge to hyperventilate.

Miklos backed away, too. A man followed him out of the bathroom. His uniform told her who he was: the general. The man had his gun aimed at Miklos's head. The scene was enough to stop her racing heart midbeat.

"It wasn't suppose to happen this way. It was supposed to go quickly and quietly," the man said, then added, "You were supposed to be spared."

She had no idea what the guy was talking about, but Miklos's eyes hardened.

"You thought you could use me after you killed my family?" he asked

"If we had a royal on our side, the royalists would have been appeased. It would have been the easiest way. You would have lost your title, but you could have gotten a high-enough post in the new cabinet."

Miklos's whole body was tense as he watched the man. He looked ready to spring forward, and she prayed that he wouldn't. No matter how quick he was, a bullet from the general's pistol would be quicker.

The man watched Miklos with mild regret on his face. "I always loved you like a son." He shook his head. "You should have been the crown prince. I could have made that work. None of this would have happened."

"You mean if I were the crown prince, you might have let me become king and tried to rule through me. We had a close relationship, which you never had with Arpad." Miklos's eyes narrowed dangerously.

The general nodded.

Tension was so thick in the room she could hardly breathe. She could do something, she told herself. She had a gun. She should do something.

But neither man paid any attention to her, as if they'd discounted her altogether. Miklos to keep the general's attention off her, she suspected, and the general because he correctly assessed the situation and knew that even without a weapon, Miklos was the more dangerous opponent.

Didn't take a genius to figure that out. He could probably see the rifle wavering with each tremor that ran down her arm.

Anger rolled off Miklos in waves. "So this is where Arpad's near misses came from. It's why his plane almost went down last month, isn't it? And that boating accident, too, had been planned?"

"Those were fully investigated and ruled accidents." The general's thin lips stretched into a syrupy smile.

"Investigated by a team you recommended," Miklos shot back and charged forward.

"Stop! Nobody moves!" Judi shouted and took one step forward, pointing the rifle at the general, wondering if she should shoot a warning round into the ceiling. Could she damage some priceless fresco, and hope that history would forgive her? She could and she would, she decided.

The general looked more amused than scared. "Drop your weapon. You're more likely to hit him than me."

He was right. Could she toss the gun to Miklos? She glanced at his damaged right hand. No way to know how good a catch he was with his left. And if she shot the ceiling, the royal guards would rush in. If the general felt trapped, he would shoot Miklos for sure.

"Let her go," Miklos bargained. "She has nothing to do with this. She's leaving the country. We're not marrying."

"Not indeed. She should have never come here. Wouldn't have come here if I had more time to arrange it. Unfortunately, her arrival was rather unexpected."

A chill ran down Judi's spine at his words. Especially when they were underscored with his cold stare.

"I always hoped you would marry my daughter," the man told Miklos casually.

Surprise flashed through Miklos's face. "She's barely twenty."

The man's raised eyebrow said that mattered little to him. He really was blinded by ambition.

"Drop your weapon." He barked his order to Judi, his eyes glinting with determination, the barrel of his pistol pushing into the skin of Miklos's forehead.

She lowered her gun, tears filling her eyes as she wished she were good enough to use it. But if she squeezed that trigger, if she hit Miklos, or if the general shot him, it would be all over. If all she gained them was a few more minutes, there was still hope that something could happen.

And it did.

Her giving up drew the general's attention from Miklos for a split second, even if it was to gloat at her.

At the same time, Miklos reached for his sword, and ran the general through in one smooth move.

Surprise crossed the man's face. But he was still standing, his finger on the trigger. And when Judi saw that finger move, she brought the rifle up and shot the man in the head.

The lucky shot of a lifetime.

It helped that by then Miklos had ducked out of the way.

When the general collapsed, she felt like she was about to follow him down to the marble tiles.

Miklos grabbed the man's gun. Then he was at Judi's side, gently removing the rifle from her trembling hand. "Take it easy, warrior princess."

The guards were bursting in from outside, weapons raised.

She barely registered them. She clung to Miklos's strength, to the thought that they were both alive, that she couldn't have lived if anything happened to him. And she knew that she would not be taking a cab to the airport anytime soon; she wouldn't be going back to Washington for a while yet. She had found something with Miklos that she had never had in D.C. She might not have known him long, but she knew all she had to know. As much as she had fought it, she had fallen in love with the prince.

Not the smartest thing she'd ever done. Even back when he did want to marry her, he'd been clear about the fact that theirs would be an arranged marriage, a marriage of convenience. Love was never under discussion. More fool she.

He could have given her castles and jewels, the life of a princess. But his love was the only thing she wanted.

LATE MORNING, WHEN the castle had been cleared of the dead and the injured, and security restored, the castle yard cleaned, Judi lay on a recliner on the balcony of one of the guest suites, wrapped in a sumptuous down comforter.

She'd been asleep already, awakened by a bad dream of bloody fighting and wanted fresh air and to look at the stars above, needed a moment of reconnecting with the universe. The past few days had been so insane that in hindsight she almost had trouble believing that they'd actually happened.

She needed to make some decisions about her future, about Miklos, and she couldn't make them inside the opulent room, which completely overwhelmed her.

And as if conjured by her thoughts, she heard his voice on the balcony beneath hers. He was talking to one of his brothers.

"She's magnificent," the brother said.

"She's mine, Benedek." Miklos's voice carried a tone of warning.

Benedek laughed. "I think I'm half in love

with her. So are Arpad and Janos and Istvan and Lazlo."

Miklos grunted. "Get your own princess."

"We're even willing to forgive her for bringing down the general." Benedek paused. "The villain should have been vanquished by one of the Brotherhood."

"She's an extraordinary woman," Miklos agreed, his words filling Judi with warmth.

"So you're in love with her?"

Judi held her breath.

But Miklos didn't answer his brother's candid question.

"I don't think I've ever been in love," Benedek mused.

Hard to believe, Judi thought. Benedek didn't have his twin brother's wild streak—with Lazlo, she had a feeling nobody knew what he might do next—but he did have that jaw-dropping, masculine gorgeousness that all the Kerkay brothers possessed. She'd seen the queen's ladies-in-waiting swarm around him earlier. But something in his voice talked of past history and regrets. His tone was too light, forced, as if manufactured to cover secrets.

And Judi was starting to feel uncomfortable. The brothers were having a private conversation. She stood slowly, without making a noise, and retreated toward the door.

The last thing she heard was Miklos saying, "Maybe you need to let go of your infatuation with that American opera-singer diva first. You need to find yourself a real woman. You're still a young pup. It can still happen."

She lay on her carved four-poster bed, feeling alone in the opulent room with its ceiling frescos of snowcapped mountains and the work-of-art crystal chandelier. The room would have made anyone feel like a princess, but she felt only uncertainty.

When Benedek had asked Miklos if he was in love with her, he hadn't responded.

And he hadn't come to her. She'd been moved into this guest suite from Miklos's bedroom by a flock of servants. That, in itself, was telling.

Not long ago, he'd told her he no longer wanted to marry her. Looked like he meant it. She squeezed her eyes shut and groaned into her pillow.

She wasn't princess material. She knew nothing about royal protocol. In fact, she hated rules and regulations. He knew it, she knew it. He was making the right decision, she tried to tell herself.

But knowing that didn't help her heart to ache any less.

He'd asked her once whether she was like the princess in her children's video games, living in her own little labyrinth. He'd meant living with limited choices. And she realized now that maybe she had been, limiting her own choices to make sure she avoided hurt and pain.

Losing her parents had been hard, but losing her stepmother had been harder still. She remembered her stepmother more than either of her biological parents and, right or wrong, missed her more. At one point she had decided that she didn't want any more loss and stopped getting attached.

The boyfriends who accused her of being commitment phobic had been right.

An arranged marriage would have been her worst nightmare—all the commitment without any of the love she craved.

MIKLOS WAS MORE THAN ready to grab some rest when Assemblyman Egon stepped in front of him. The man had rushed to the castle to have an emergency meeting with Arpad in the wake of the night's violence. Egon had been Chancellor Hansen's right-hand man, very likely the person who would replace him.

"A word, Your Highness." Tall as a beanpole, with the eyes of a fox, he stood squarely in front of the prince. Daring, but the new chancellor would need that quality.

"Tomorrow." Miklos stepped around him and kept walking.

The assemblyman fell in step beside him. "I understand the Lady Judit is still in the castle."

"She's resting."

"Have any commitments been made?"

"No."

"Good." His sigh of relief was audible. "The Assembly has been considering, Your Highness. She might not be the right choice. In fact, we believe she is not. It has always been only Chancellor Hansen who pushed her as the best candidate."

"Chancellor Hansen died last night for this country," Miklos reminded the man sharply, not liking the direction the conversation was taking.

"Forgive me." The man had the good sense to look chastised. "But the issue of the Lady Judit—"

"Is my decision entirely."

"Certainly, Your Highness. I'm merely suggesting that the general's daughter—"

"Are you jesting?" They reached the staircase and Miklos stopped to face the man.

"The general's death, coming at the same time as Chancellor Hansen's, will shake the country. There will be fear of retribution for the rebellion. If the monarchy is seen as too heavy-handed… A gesture of forgiveness would be best, Your Highness. And the general's daughter is a native daughter of our country. She is dedicated to youth and charity."

"She *is* a youth. She wants to marry me?" he asked incredulously. "I rather imagine the girl would be grieving."

"After a suitable period of mourning, of course. She will be persuaded that the marriage would be the best thing. She will do her duty, I'm sure, to save her family from disgrace."

"Her father's actions are no disgrace of hers."

"Certainly, Your Highness. And your understanding will raise your popularity among the people. I knew… The Assembly is confident that you will do your duty. I will make arrangements for the Lady Judit to be returned to her home before the day is out."

"You will not."

"Your Highness, duty—"

"Duty be damned." He turned his back to the man and took the steps two at a time to see Judi.

HER THOUGHTS DRIFTED to all she and Miklos had survived together in the last couple of days. Whatever happened next, the most important thing was that he was alive. He'd fought in the terrifying battle to take back the castle, and he'd made it.

He was a warrior prince.

He was the kind of man daydreams were made of.

He could have been hers. She could have been his.

Don't think about that. If she could fall in love against her will, then, maybe, if she worked hard enough, she could fall out of it.

He liked her, but not enough to overlook the fact that she'd make a lousy princess.

He'd told her as much after they'd made love in the general's prison. But despite that, she couldn't regret that night. At least she would have those memories of him. Her mind went back to those heated and all-too-brief moments between them. She was tired to the bone. Her thoughts drifted, her body still exhausted. Judi was nearly asleep again by the time a muted knock sounded on her door.

"Come in."

"Did I wake you?" Miklos stopped, his silhouette tall and wide-shouldered, just inside her bedroom door.

Her heart started into an erratic rhythm. She shook her head with a nervous smile.

"Sorry I didn't come sooner. I took the chopper to the hospital. Dr. Arynak wouldn't let me rest until I had the hand checked out."

"How is it?" She sat up in bed.

"The bullet went through. One of the bones

shattered, but not too badly. They put the pieces back together." He came closer.

She noticed the fresh, white bandage. Relief filled her. She'd been worried about that. "They let you leave?"

"They weren't given a choice. I had to come back to talk to you," he said softly, reaching her bed. His eyes were dark with unnamed emotions.

Her heart clamored in her chest.

He reached out his good hand and cupped her face. "I'm sorry you were drawn into this mess. I can't stand the thought that something could have happened to you." He was leaning toward her.

She still couldn't say anything, and when his lips touched hers, her last coherent thoughts disappeared.

His kiss and touch were gentle. She let him lay her back down onto the silk sheets, and moaned in pleasure when his body covered hers.

He pulled away only long enough to remove the comforter from between them. Then raised an eyebrow as he took her in.

She wore some antique reproduction of a princess nightgown, made of white silk and lace. One of the maids had given it to her. In the early morning sunlight that poured in the window, the gown left little to the imagination.

She felt self-conscious all of a sudden as her nipples puckered under his heated gaze. And since he was the kind of guy who rarely missed anything, he caught that and focused on them. A sexy smile spread across his lips.

"You should have come to Valtria sooner." His mouth brushing a nipple through the silk took away her ability to answer.

His good hand ran up under the gown, caressing her heated skin. She arched against him in wanton need as she kneaded his shoulders.

"I don't think you should be princess," he said.

Her heart sank. Here it came. She needed to steel herself and be reasonable. He was one hundred percent right about this. She hated that the words hurt anyway.

"You grew up with different ideals. A lot more freedom. It would be hard on you. More than I can ask."

Her breath caught in her throat.

"But I'm going to ask it anyway. I don't want you to go," he said.

She was too stunned for a second, needing a gulp of air before she could respond. "I won't," she breathed.

"I mean not ever."

Her gaze locked with his.

"I want you to marry me," he went on. "I

know that for you this seems too old-fashioned and too sudden, but—"

She reached up and silenced him with a kiss. Her heart sang. Her body was shaky with need.

Long minutes passed before they separated again.

"Marriage to me…I can't guarantee that I'll be worth the trouble, no matter how hard I'll try," he made a point to tell her.

"You're worth it."

He grinned. "I love you." Then he turned all serious, and said, "I love you" again.

"I love you, too, Prince Miklos."

"Princess Judi." He tasted the words. "I'm going to love saying that."

He kissed her before she could respond. And, really, what response was there to give? What they had between them was pure joy, pure love, a gift from heaven.

"I'm sorry I don't have a ring. I want something of historical significance, but the most important royal jewels are kept in the treasury. Even I have to make an appointment to take something out."

"I don't need a fancy ring."

"You'll have a ring that'll be the envy of princesses around the world."

"You just want everyone within a mile to know that I belong to you."

"I suppose you haven't called me archaic in days, so I was due for a reminder." His eyes danced. "But you do speak the truth. You belong to me." He turned thoughtful. "Do you think we could have a T-shirt made? Aren't those things a custom in your country?"

She swatted at him playfully. Then she thought of something and giggled.

He pulled back. "What is it?"

"To think that I almost went to Puerto Vallarta instead."

"Why didn't you?"

"Aunt Viola talked me out of it. She said they had lizards, and giant spiders, and snakes and bats."

"At the resort?" His voice was skeptical.

"In hindsight, she might have exaggerated. She was adamant that I should come here."

"I'll see to it that she receives a royal commendation."

"Oh, she would like that."

"Do you know what I would like?"

She grinned. "From the look in your eyes, I have a couple of pretty good guesses."

His smile turned wolfish. "I do love smart princesses."

"Just the one, I hope."

"I love *my* princess," he corrected. "I love you, Judi Marezzi, soon to be Kerkay." He gave a low growl deep in his throat. "Can't be soon enough for me."

The kiss he gave her made her head spin. His hand worshipped every inch of her body, removing all obstacles.

The sun bathed the room in golden light.

He was naked.

Wow.

Magnificent.

They'd been partially undressed when they'd made love at the general's compound, thinking that might be their last day alive, but their prison had been nearly pitch-dark. This was the first time she could really see him.

She let her gaze glide over the smooth hills and valleys of his body. Everything in perfect order and then some. Wide chest, flat abdomen with ripples of muscles in orderly rows. Even his body looked disciplined.

She reached out. His skin was warm beneath her hand. She could feel the steady beating of his heart.

She leaned forward, brushed her lips against his. "I didn't want this to happen."

"I did," he said matter-of-factly and grabbed her hips to fit her to him.

"Since when?" She pulled her head back to look into his eyes.

"Since you walked off the plane."

Satisfaction, pleasure, vanity—or something akin to those—thrilled through her.

"I thought you were airport security."

He gave a short bark of a laugh at that.

And kissed her hard. And somehow maneuvered her to right where he wanted her. Then began the slow process of seducing her body, touch by touch, nibble by nibble, driving her to the edge with his seemingly endless patience. But he made her wait, made her hotter with every touch, made her need him.

He was perfect. He was her prince. He loved her. Her head was spinning. He touched her so tenderly that it made her heart ache. She couldn't keep her roaming hands from exploring him.

She needed him to blot out the images of the violence of the last couple of days. She wanted to do the same for him. She wanted to make him forget his injury.

"Shouldn't you be careful with your hand?"

"They shot me with enough painkillers that I won't have any feeling in it for at least another hour. I want to take full advantage of that hour. The rest of my body has plenty of feeling in it. I'm thinking we should focus on the positive."

She laid him down on the bed. "Let's just keep the hand out of harm's way."

"Will you play nurse to your wounded soldier?" His wolfish grin widened.

"You bet." She bent to kiss him. She loved his sensuous, masculine mouth.

That mouth could make her do just about anything, she reflected long moments later, her body vibrating with tension and pleasure.

He shifted their positions and turned her under him, supporting himself above her on his elbows, bringing his good hand up to her chin as he dipped his head to kiss her again.

His corded muscles betrayed that he was as much on the edge as she was, but he held back, took his time with her. He trailed kisses down her cheek, her neck, moving with excruciating slowness toward a peaking nipple that begged for his attentions. He heard the silent call and proved to be extraordinarily accommodating.

He seemed to know what she wanted and when, in exactly which way. Heat pulsed between her legs where their bodies touched, and she could feel his hard desire. Her knees came up; her legs wrapped around him.

Now. She wanted him now, all of him. She'd never wanted anyone or anything with such desperate urgency.

But he took his time with her other nipple, melting the bones in her body. Now. Now. Now. She couldn't take much more of this. Patience was a virtue she was momentarily missing.

"Please," she whispered.

He moved to the underside of her breast, then trailed hot kisses lower and lower.

She lost the ability to breathe.

And then they made sweet love to each other, the princess and the prince.

Epilogue

"How is my Princess Judi?" Miklos came up behind her and wrapped his arms around her growing belly as she checked her hair, which the royal stylist had prepared to perfection an hour earlier. "I can't wait to hold our baby."

"You and me both. He's been pretty active today. I swear he's practicing fencing in there."

"Never too early to start. Ready to go?"

"Sure." Going to dinner at the royal palace still put butterflies in her stomach, though. Buckingham Palace in London had nothing on the royal palace of Valtria, which was majestic in both size and splendor. She still hadn't gotten used to the army of servants in residence. Her own ancestral castle at the foot of the mountains seemed more manageable by comparison, although she was still overwhelmed even by that. For now the castle was all she could handle.

She wasn't quite ready for palace life yet, with all its studied formality and protocol. To her surprise, she'd found the royal family more than accommodating—even the queen, who'd found new strength in the news that she would soon have a grandchild. Her condition had turned for the better. She was determined to see the baby born.

Since the princes often visited Maltmore Castle, her nearest neighbor now, keeping an eye on restorations, they had plenty of company. The country was calm, and she hoped it would stay this way forever. The general was dead, the rebel forces dispersed.

She tried not to think of the few remaining dissenters or the Freedom Council and the three powerful men who formed it, none of whom had been unmasked yet. Miklos was working on that still. And she had full confidence in her husband. He was the most wonderful man she'd ever known. She loved her life here.

Truth was, Judi was being spoiled rotten. The princes fawned over her and flirted with her outrageously, sometimes just to get Miklos's goat. The queen treated her like the beloved daughter she'd never had.

Her head spun from this sudden large loving family. They truly were extraordinary, in every sense of the word. She hoped the little stunt she'd just pulled wouldn't get any of them mad at her.

"What?" Miklos caught the look on her face immediately.

"I just…" She hesitated. "How does Benedek feel about meddling?"

"In what?" Miklos's eyes narrowed.

"His love life," she said on a thin voice, thinking that what she'd done might not have been the best idea she'd ever had.

"What have you done?" Miklos held her closer.

"The renovations on the Royal Opera House are done."

"Correct." He watched her closely.

"And it needs a fitting opening night."

"Since when are you interested in the opera?"

"Since I asked Rayne to give the opening performance." She held her breath.

"Rayne Williams?"

She nodded, impressed that he would know the woman's last name. The reigning diva of opera had gone by first name only in the past decade. At age forty, she was hailed as the biggest sensation of the century. Her beauty inspired movies and lines of cosmetics. And apparently a young European prince.

"Do you think Benedek will kill me? He's had a crush on her forever." Which he tried to keep a secret, but couldn't quite hide. Not when he would drop everything and fly wherever she was to see each of her new performances.

"If she still traveled, he would probably have invited her himself. Don't be too disappointed if she says no," Miklos warned.

The diva's paralyzing fear of flying was public knowledge. Five years before, her mother and brother had died in a plane crash. The only reason she hadn't been on the plane was because of a vocal-cord injury that had needed immediate medical assistance. Her manager had switched her flight to the next one, then rushed her to a specialist. She didn't make that flight, either, nor any other since.

"She's doing much better," Judi reassured him.

"And how do you know this?"

"Aunt Viola."

"Is she ever coming to Valtria?"

"Maybe for the christening. She's still too nervous to go before the queen. She thinks she might be reprimanded for neglecting her duties around me for the last two decades."

Miklos's only response was rolling his eyes toward the ceiling. "How does Aunt Viola know Rayne?" he asked then, as if on second thought.

"Rayne's mother was a good friend to her. They were on some charity boards together. She kept in touch with the daughter."

"I thought her job in the U.S. was to watch over you, not to socialize."

"I hardly needed full-time supervision."

A dark eyebrow lifted slightly. "I beg to differ. You've certainly been a handful ever since you got here. I can't take my eyes off you for a second."

She nudged an elbow into the solid wall of muscle behind her.

"Okay." He gave up teasing her. "If Aunt Viola can get Rayne to come to Valtria and make my little brother happy, I'll have an official letter of pardon issued by the queen for all her past and future sins."

She turned in his arms and caught her breath at the full-of-love look he gave her.

"Hey, it's turning out to be a pretty good year." He dipped to brush his mouth over hers. "The queen is feeling better than she has in a long time. We managed to stop a rebellion. I found the love of my life, and Benedek's about to get a chance at his, and Istvan—" He snapped his mouth shut.

"What about Istvan?"

"I just meant that he's about to become an uncle. All my brothers are. And they're all very excited." He nibbled her lower lip.

And almost distracted her enough to forget what they were talking about. Almost.

She pulled back. "What about Istvan?"

He looked uncomfortable. "I'm not supposed to say."

"He's in love, too?" The man was such an introvert. She would be curious about the woman who brought that one to his knees. He spent most of his time in museums and writing historical papers for the Royal Academy. He did some digs, too. He was sort of like Indiana Jones, but much more handsome, and much, much more geeky.

"Love? God, no." Miklos looked at her in horror. "She would have to be at least a thousand years old and come in a sarcophagus in mint condition to get my brother interested."

"He found something?" she guessed.

He nodded reluctantly. She'd seen that look before.

"This wouldn't have something to do with the mysterious Brotherhood of the Crown, would it?"

He gave her an infuriating, noncommittal grin.

"Let me guess, he found the graves of the original princes."

"Oh, we know where those are. In the catacombs under the Abbey."

"He found their legendary swords?"

Regret clouded his eyes immediately. "Those are still lost."

Her eyes went wide with her next thought. "He found the jewels?"

According to legend, which she'd had plenty of time to research lately, the original Brotherhood's romantic conquests were secondary only to their fighting skills. And the ladies who were in love with them, supposedly numbering in the thousands—although she found that hard to believe—tended to gift them with tokens of their appreciation, mostly a piece of their jewels, as keepsakes or good-luck charms or whatever. By all accounts, the hoard they'd accumulated had been considerable.

They'd planned to finance an army with it and push out foreign invaders, but they were betrayed and killed, and their treasure disappeared.

"He found the jewels?" she asked again when Miklos wouldn't respond.

"He found some papers that might lead him to the jewels," Miklos admitted at last, reluctantly. "You know how part of the ceiling came down in the guardhouse at the base of the South Tower during the fight?"

"I'm not likely to forget that, since I was right under it."

His arms tightened around her. "Istvan went out there the day after, looking for clues of medieval construction and hoping he might find some broken tools or weapons that had been walled in. He found a leather pouch with some papers."

"Well, what do they say?"

"Nothing. Mold had about eaten all the way through them. But he's convinced he found a clue."

He would be. Istvan was nothing if not optimistic about the slightest find, no matter how trivial. Of course, he would think it was some important clue. And he was probably equally convinced that he could restore those papers somehow and read them. The man had singular focus when it came to his work.

"Don't tell them you know about this." Miklos kissed one of her eyelids first, then the other. "The Brotherhood's supposed to be our secret thing," he said in a tone as if he were talking about mischievous kids. Like it was all his brothers' doing. Like he didn't get a huge kick out of their secret meetings and all this.

She smiled. God, she loved her valiant, secret-society prince. "My lips are sealed."

He kissed her. "Could we wait with that for a few more minutes?"

* * * * *

millsandboon.co.uk Community

Join Us!

The Community is the perfect place to meet and chat to kindred spirits who love books and reading as much as you do, but it's also the place to:

- **Get the inside scoop from authors about their latest books**
- **Learn how to write a romance book with advice from our editors**
- **Help us to continue publishing the best in women's fiction**
- **Share your thoughts on the books we publish**
- **Befriend other users**

Forums: Interact with each other as well as authors, editors and a whole host of other users worldwide.

Blogs: Every registered community member has their own blog to tell the world what they're up to and what's on their mind.

Book Challenge: We're aiming to read 5,000 books and have joined forces with The Reading Agency in our inaugural Book Challenge.

Profile Page: Showcase yourself and keep a record of your recent community activity.

Social Networking: We've added buttons at the end of every post to share via digg, Facebook, Google, Yahoo, technorati and de.licio.us.

www.millsandboon.co.uk